"Carson   **pen."**

"A ride isn't

"No, this," s   rself and
back to him.

"Right, of course we aren't." He walked around her horse and was suddenly at her side. "I'm asking you to go for a ride. An hour or two of relaxation, not worrying about all the stuff piling up on us. I could use that break."

She closed her eyes and prayed for strength. "Carson."

When she opened her eyes he was still in front of her, his smile a little bit sweet and a little bit rakish. "Yes?"

"Why are you doing this?"

"Simple. We have unfinished business, Ruby. You left and I've spent a lot of years wondering why."

"Because I wasn't good for you," she whispered. "We were young and making decisions that would have…"

"Changed everything?" he asked. "Because I've thought about that a lot over the years. My life would have been different if you'd been in it."

"Mine, too," she admitted.

* * *

Lone Star Cowboy League:
Bighearted ranchers in small-town Texas

Brenda Minton lives in the Ozarks with her husband, children, cats, dogs and strays. She is a pastor's wife, Sunday school teacher, coffee addict and sleep-deprived. Not in that order. Her dream to be an author for Harlequin started somewhere in the pages of a romance novel about a young American woman stranded in a Spanish castle. Her dreams came true, and twenty-plus books later, she is an author hoping to inspire young girls to dream.

Books by Brenda Minton

Love Inspired

Lone Star Cowboy League

A Reunion for the Rancher

Martin's Crossing

A Rancher for Christmas
The Rancher Takes a Bride
The Rancher's Second Chance

Cooper Creek

Christmas Gifts
"Her Christmas Cowboy"
The Cowboy's Holiday Blessing
The Bull Rider's Baby
The Rancher's Secret Wife
The Cowboy's Healing Ways
The Cowboy Lawman
The Cowboy's Christmas Courtship
The Cowboy's Reunited Family
Single Dad Cowboy

Visit the Author Profile page at Harlequin.com for more titles.

A Reunion
for the Rancher

Brenda Minton

HARLEQUIN® LOVE INSPIRED®

Special thanks and acknowledgment to Brenda Minton
for her contribution to the Lone Star Cowboy League miniseries.

Recycling programs
for this product may
not exist in your area.

™ LOVE INSPIRED BOOKS

ISBN-13: 978-0-373-81864-8

A Reunion for the Rancher

www.Harlequin.com

Printed in U.S.A.

For I know the thoughts that I think toward you,
says the Lord, thoughts of peace and not of evil,
to give you a future and a hope.
—*Jeremiah* 29:11

To my kids

To Josh and Brooke,
for the love you share now and the love that will continue to grow between you. I love you both.

Luke, I love you and I'm dedicating a book to you.

Hanna, you are beautiful and talented and I love you.

Chapter One

Carson Thorn parked his truck in front of the rock-sided building that housed offices of the Little Horn, Texas, chapter of the Lone Star Cowboy League. As distracted as he was, he couldn't help but think about the history of the century-old group. It had started as a service organization, serving communities and ranchers across the state. Today it felt more like the last line of defense for ranchers who were being hit hard by thieves. The cattle rustling had started a month ago and showed no signs of letting up.

At today's meeting the other members were expecting answers. They wanted him to come up with solutions. He wished he had some. And he wished he was anywhere else on a Thursday in October than in town at this meeting.

He grabbed his briefcase and locked his

truck. As he did, he noticed a white sedan pull into another parking space. He didn't stop to see who it might be. He had paperwork to hand over to the league secretary, and Byron McKay, one of the biggest ranchers in the state, was waiting to talk to him. That wasn't a conversation Carson looked forward to. He never looked forward to talking to Byron. Knowing that Byron's ranch had recently been hit by the thieves, Carson knew the conversation wouldn't be pleasant. This was one of those days when he wished he could live in a community and not be involved.

Someone must have been looking out for him, giving him one thing to be thankful for. Ingrid Edwards, the league secretary, wasn't at her desk. He sighed with relief. One bullet dodged. Now he just had to face Byron. The older man was already seated in the boardroom, a stack of papers in front of him.

"Byron." Carson pulled off the sport coat he'd worn and tossed it on the back of his chair. He rolled up his sleeves and then poured himself a glass of water.

"This has to be stopped, Carson." Byron pushed himself out of his chair and shed his own jacket. The rancher, a little paunchy and with thinning, strawberry blond hair, managed to knock over his own water glass.

Carson tossed him a roll of paper towels. He wasn't playing maid to anyone, not even a McKay. He cringed, thinking of Byron's offspring, twin teenaged boys who were sure to be chips off the old block someday.

He gave the other man a careful look, not wanting to wade too far in.

"I'm aware that it has to stop, Byron. I'm not sure what you want me personally to do about it. Do you want me on patrol? Do you want me to guard your livestock?"

"We need a plan. And maybe some of us do need to patrol. Lucy Benson is a great sheriff, but I'm not sure she's up to snuff on this case."

"Lucy is just fine." Carson sat down in his chair at the end of the table. Times like this he'd like it if someone else was the local chapter president.

"Well, I for one think that Derek Donovan should be questioned."

"Why do you think that?" Carson asked the question, but he knew the answer.

"Because he got out of prison and that's when all of this started." McKay slammed his meaty fist on the top of the table.

"Stop blaming my grandson," a shaky voice said from the open door.

Carson rubbed a hand over his face and groaned. "Iva."

"Yes, Iva." The older woman pushed her walker into the room. "I'm still a member, Carson Thorn, and don't you forget that."

"No one is forgetting." Carson stood and went to her side to pull out a chair for her. She was nearing eighty, and in the past few months, Parkinson's had started to take a toll on her health. But Iva wasn't letting it stop her, not until she didn't have a say in the matter.

She waved him away, not taking the offered chair. "I'm not feeling the best, so I'm not staying for the meeting. I just wanted to confront you all and tell you this neighbor-blaming-neighbor business has to stop."

Byron McKay faced the woman, his tone only slightly more gentle. "I've lost more cattle and equipment, Iva. My boys lost a couple of dirt bikes. This thief knows us and knows our ranches."

Iva shook her head and raised a frail hand that jerked as she pointed an unsteady finger at the rancher. Her arm trembled as she tried to steady the gesture, adding a fierce glare that had Carson smiling. No one could beat down Iva Donovan. Even with her failing health she was a force to be reckoned with.

"Watch how you talk about my family, you bully in a Stetson."

"I'm not running you down, Iva. You've had it tough and none of us blames you."

"If you blame my kin, you blame me." She shook her head at the chair Carson offered. "My grandson made mistakes and paid for those crimes. I'll not have you pointing fingers at him."

"Iva, you know we have to look at everyone in a situation like this," Carson said, hoping he sounded diplomatic and not as suspicious as he really felt.

"We don't have to start accusing our neighbors or searching their homes and farms," Iva argued. She rested heavily on the walker as she looked from Carson to the other members who were trickling in. "Don't come to my place again unless you have real evidence."

Carson shot Byron McKay a warning look that silenced him. "Iva, unless they have a reason, they won't search your place."

"They don't have a reason," Iva insisted with a growl. "And you aren't going to harass my family."

"No, Iva, we won't do that." Carson took charge because he could see Iva weakening as her anger took over. She'd always been a spitfire and having Parkinson's hadn't taken any of her orneriness away, just her energy. "We've got the police on this and our own investigation team. We're putting up surveillance cameras. We'll figure out who's responsible."

"I hope you do," she said a little more calmly. "Now I have to go, so you all continue on without me."

"Let me walk you out to your car," he offered.

"Hey, we still have things to discuss. You're the chapter president and you can't just walk out, Carson," Byron McKay bellowed.

"Byron, relax. I'm walking Iva to her car and I'll be back." Carson reached for the door, and Iva smiled up at him. Her blue eyes were faded and rimmed with red, but she winked and he saw that spunk that had gotten her through some tough times.

"Byron McKay has more bluster than sense," Iva snipped as they walked out of the meeting room.

"He does tend to go on." He helped Iva through the main room and headed her toward the doors.

He nodded at Ingrid Edwards, once again behind her desk. She was shuffling through a drawer but she smiled up at him, her glasses sliding down her nose and red hair coming loose from a clip that held it to the top of her head. She winked and he wasn't quite sure what to do.

Last week she'd brought him fried chicken. The week before that, brownies. Ingrid was on the prowl, looking for a husband before she turned twenty-six. Or so the rumor went. He didn't want to hurt her feelings, but she'd have to look elsewhere. He was thirty-one and had no intention of settling down.

"It isn't my Derek," Iva muttered as they headed for the front door. "I know you think you know him, Carson Thorn, but you don't. He's a changed boy."

"He's almost twenty, Iva. That's not really a boy."

"He's still my boy and I won't let you or anyone else run him down. I appreciate what you've done over the years, but when it comes to family, I draw the line."

"As you should."

She stopped just feet short of the door, leaning heavily on the walker. She studied him with those blue eyes of hers. "I've always appreciated your help."

"My help?"

"The lawyer, for Derek."

He cleared his throat and glanced out the door, hoping to avoid a conversation he didn't want to have. But she wouldn't let it go.

"Johnny Mac fixing my truck," Iva continued. "And that beef in my fridge."

"We should go. I need to get in there before Byron and the others really do form a posse like they've been discussing. We can't have them riding off on horses, guns blazing."

She laughed a gravely sounding laugh. "Your daddy was made of the same cloth as that Byron McKay. You're a different breed. Don't be like them."

"I try not to be."

"You ain't been to church in a good long while."

He should have known it would come back to that. "I've been busy."

"Oh, land's sakes, don't give me that. I'm not sure what burr got under your saddle, but it isn't so big that God can't fix it."

He smiled and shook his head. "I know He's capable. But there's no burr, just a busy life."

"Help me to my car, then."

They were on the sidewalk heading for the old Buick Iva drove. And that's when he saw Ruby Donovan. She stood in front of the white car dressed in shorts, canvas sneakers and a T-shirt. Her auburn hair lifted slightly in the breeze and she pushed it back and held it with her hand as she watched him approach. Seeing her like that took him back to the first time he'd seen her. She'd been fifteen. He'd been seventeen. She'd just gotten off some crazy ride at the county fair. She'd been laughing at something her friend had said and walking toward the Ferris wheel.

Today felt a lot like that moment when they'd met. And nothing like that moment. Today when she looked at him her hazel eyes didn't sparkle. Her mouth didn't form that generous smile. No, she glared. He felt more than a little edgy seeing her up close and in person for the first time in twelve years.

One of these days he'd like to get an answer from her. He'd like to know what he'd done to deserve her walking away without even saying goodbye. He'd like to know how she'd gone from wanting to spend a life together to wanting nothing more than a free ride to college, compliments of his father.

But maybe it was better if he didn't know.

Ruby sucked in a breath and tried to pretend her heart wasn't tripping all over itself the way it had always tripped when she saw Carson Thorn. She'd managed to avoid him for a dozen years. That hadn't been easy considering he lived just down the road from her grandmother. But somehow on her odd trips home she'd managed.

But seeing him, the tall rancher with the dark brown hair and brown eyes that a girl could get lost in, was like going back. It was like being in love again. And she wasn't in love. He was no longer that boy, and she was no longer an impressionable teenage girl who believed in happy-ever-after.

It was this man who had taken those dreams from her. This man and his family. Until she'd met the Thorns she had always been good enough.

To see him helping her Gran to the car, that sizzled down deep where the red in her hair lived waiting to be unleashed.

She stepped forward, ignoring the confused look on his face. She ignored expensive cologne that smelled like the mountains and the ocean and everything good in between. She tried, desperately, to ignore the fact that the air seemed too thick to breathe when he was in her space. The need for oxygen meant she had to get him gone as quickly as possible.

"Thank you, Carson. I'll help her to the car."

"Be nice, Ruby Jo," Iva warned.

"I'm being nice." Ruby stepped close to help her grandmother off the sidewalk.

Iva leaned in. "No, you're showing your claws. You have no idea, Ruby."

"I have ideas." She looked back. Carson was still there, watching them.

Her younger brother, Derek, was nowhere to

be found. He'd said something about errands to run and he'd get a ride home. She didn't like when he disappeared. She trusted him, but since cattle had started disappearing just a little too close to the time Derek had been released from prison, she knew he was going to continue to be a suspect until someone was caught.

These days everyone was a suspect.

She was surprised no one had tried to blame *her* since she'd arrived back in town only a few weeks ago.

Carson interrupted her thoughts, and that was too bad because she'd been trying to block him from her mind and her memories. He stepped past her and opened the car door.

Once Iva was situated, Ruby took her purse out of the walker and folded the contraption up to store it in the trunk of the car. She turned, and Carson Thorn was there. Without a word, he took the walker from her hands. If she'd trusted herself to speak, she would have told him that she could take care of things herself.

Funny that his name was Thorn, because he was a real thorn in her side. A thorn she'd prayed like the apostle Paul that God would remove from her. She'd tried to pray away his memory. And now? She didn't need him lurking, being kind, respectful. She needed him to go away and not be a reminder of everything she'd lost and why she'd left Little Horn.

If it hadn't been for Iva and Derek, she would have stayed in Oklahoma, and then she wouldn't have had this issue to deal with. But she was home. And they did need her here. Her grandmother needed her.

"Is that frown for me?"

What should she say to that? She could say, of course it wasn't. Or she could admit that it was. "I didn't realize I was frowning."

He leaned against the back of the car, long legs in new jeans and those expensive boots of his. The walker was still in his hands.

"You were definitely frowning."

"I should have sold the ranch and convinced Gran and Derek to move to Oklahoma with me," she admitted without intending to.

"What would have been the fun in that? You're not a city girl, Ruby. You were born and raised in Hill Country, and you can't outrun it."

"I've been living in the city a long time, and I'm adaptable."

His smile faded. "Yes, I guess you are."

She wondered about that smile, why he acted as if it was all about him. She wondered if he had any clue how much his dad and sister had hurt her. How much he'd hurt her? It wasn't as if she'd wanted to stay gone from her home. She'd stayed gone because she hadn't been able to imagine seeing him with someone else. She was only back because Gran's health had deteriorated and someone had to look out for Derek.

"Listen, we don't have to do this. When we see each other, we don't have to get tugged back into the past. It was a long time ago and I'm over it. I'm sure you're over it since…" She shook her head. She wasn't going there. "I have work to do."

He stepped away from the back of the car and pointed, indicating she should open the trunk. When she did, he lifted the walker and stowed it inside. "There you go. Is there anything else you need help with?"

She stared up at the tall, overpowering rancher, surprised by the offer. She tried to see the boy she'd known in the face of this ruggedly handsome stranger. The features were stronger, more defined, more…everything. His eyes were shuttered against emotion. But she saw a flicker, maybe a hint of warmth.

"I don't need help. We've always gotten along just fine."

"Did you put up the surveillance cameras the league handed out?"

"I have them in a box. I haven't had a chance

to take them out, and I don't know if I can do it myself."

"I can help you put them up."

She wondered if her mouth had dropped when he made that offer. Purposefully, she clamped her lips and shook her head. "I'll read the directions and do it myself," she insisted. Yes, she knew the only difference between her and a stubborn five-year-old was the lack of a foot stomp on her part.

"I was trying to help."

"I know. And I really do appreciate that. But I can take care of things. Derek will help me." She put a finger up and wagged it in his face. "Don't say it."

He grinned and suddenly the tension in the air melted just a little. "I won't say it. But if you change your mind, let me know."

"I will." She took a few steps away from him, feeling better with the solid metal of the sedan between them.

"It's been nice talking to you, Ruby."

With that, he walked away.

"Yes, nice talking to you." Nice going back in time and revisiting heartache. And the other leftover emotions. The ones that should have been long gone—feelings she hadn't expected to surface after so many years. Ruby stood there for too long, and a car honked. She stepped out of the way, waving absently at the car pulling into the parking space next to hers.

She opened the door of the sedan and climbed in behind the wheel. She glanced at her passenger, and Iva pretended not to be grinning.

"Gran, do not get that look on your face. Carson Thorn is twelve years in my past. I can do without him and without his daddy's money."

"His daddy has been gone a few years, honey."

"Yes, I know that."

"And you have to think about forgiving, because hanging on to all that resentment isn't good for a soul. While you're at it, forgive his sister."

She started the Buick and glanced quickly at her granny before shifting the car into Reverse. "How do you know about Jenna?"

"As if there are any secrets in this town. You didn't want to tell me, but I heard that she said some things about you not being the right woman for her brother and that he'd found someone in college that would make him a perfect wife. A woman who didn't buy her clothes at the thrift store."

"I didn't want you to know. It would have…"

"Hurt me? No, not at all. We did the best we

could, and there's no shame in buying clothes secondhand. It's called being good stewards of what God gives us."

She swiped at the tear trickling down her cheek and reached for her grandmother's hand. "You are so important to me."

"I know." Iva grinned and squeezed her hand. "Now, let's get on out to the house, and you try to stop thinking about Carson Thorn."

Stop thinking about Carson. Of course. She would just put his memory aside. She would forget summer days at the lake, two kids in love planning their future, the house they would build, the horses they would raise together.

They'd been kids planning a way to conquer the world and their own pasts.

His past: the death of his mom in his early teens and a dad who wouldn't accept anything less than perfection.

Her past: the loss of her mom and then her dad. There had been a lot of dysfunction before they'd been turned over to their granny Iva to raise.

Life had brought her full circle, back to Little Horn, back to Iva and Derek. She would try to start a new life in Little Horn, working with kids, giving riding lessons and maybe rebuilding the farm.

Carson Thorn wouldn't even cross her mind. Not if she stayed busy, stayed clear of town and never stepped foot off the ranch. If she had no social life and no friends, she would never bump into him.

"I wonder why he never married?" The question slipped out, totally unintended. "You know, the woman he met. Did he ever bring her around?"

Iva shot her a knowing look. "You know, for years you haven't let me mention him. Why all of the questions now?"

"Just curious."

"I never saw him with another woman, Ruby. He's worked the ranch, tried to keep that sister of his out of trouble and he's done his best for the town."

Ruby shrugged it off. "Not that I care."

"Of course you don't."

"I do not care." Ruby turned on to the driveway that led to the Donovan ranch. A long driveway with sagging fences running along both sides. At the end of the drive sat a white farm house and a sagging barn to match those fences.

When she looked at her home she saw work that should have been done years ago. She saw neglect.

She should have come home more often. She

should have ignored her grandmother's claims that everything was fine. Somehow she'd convinced herself that the money she sent home was needed more than her presence. Random weekends home hadn't been enough to keep things going, though.

"Stop beating yourself up, Ruby." Iva reached to open her door, but she paused to give Ruby a sharp look. "It was my choice to let Slim go. I just couldn't see paying him anymore. And it was me who told you that we could get by."

"I should have come home." Ruby let her gaze slide over the landscape, the fields dotted with a few head of cattle, the hills in the distance and the blue, blue sky rising above it. "I love this place."

And she'd let heartache keep her from it, from the people she loved and the life she loved. But she was back now, and she would make this ranch profitable again.

She hoped it wasn't too little, too late, because she wouldn't run again. She would face the past and face Carson Thorn. Even if it hurt.

Chapter Two

As much as Carson loved living on this ranch in Texas Hill Country, some mornings he'd just as soon put it on the market and move to the city. Or to another country. This was one of those mornings. He'd been up since well before daybreak, and he'd heard nothing but problems and complaints since he set foot in the barn.

The hay they'd bought from Iowa hadn't showed up, there was an outbreak of pinkeye and someone really needed to do something about the wild hogs that were tearing up a section of field at the back of the property where the hills were steep and a creek supplied water. Carson poured himself a cup of coffee, raised a hand to the young kid about to ask what he needed to do, since it was his second day on the job, and walked out the back of the barn to watch the sun come up over an autumn landscape.

He sighed as he sipped about the worst coffee in history. For a brief moment he could forget wild hogs, pinkeye, drought and cattle thieves. For that moment, as he watched the sun come up, he knew God existed and he knew that as bad as things could look, somehow they always worked out in the end. For a man who sometimes felt as far from God as he could get, maybe that was getting somewhere.

The door creaked open. He sighed and turned to face that kid again. Ron? No. Rolland? Rick.

"Can I help you, Rick?"

"I just thought I should tell you that gray mare of yours looks like she's got a tendon problem. I've doctored her the best I could, but I think she might need a vet. And…" The kid let out a breath as if that was how he filled himself with courage. "Someone got into the trophy case. This back door was open when I got here."

"Trophy case?" Why would anyone want trophies that were thirty years old?

"There are a few empty spaces and some belt buckles missing." Rick cleared his throat on that news. "I'm sorry."

"I'll take a look. I can't imagine anything of value. Just dusty old trophies. Keepsakes, mostly."

"Maybe the silver?"

"I guess a few of them might have silver." He followed Rick inside. "Did Larry and Gayla show up to take that gelding and the other mare to the show in Houston?"

"Yes, sir. They left last night. Larry wanted to get them there a few days early, give them time to settle in before the event."

That's why Larry was his trainer. The couple was invaluable. They trained, they were able to hit shows and rodeos he couldn't, and they were dependable.

Rick, just eighteen, tall and wiry with a shock of wheat-colored hair, led him to the tack and trophy room. He pointed to the trophy case, his face a little pale. Carson stepped close, surveying the loss. It wasn't much, a few trophies, mostly sentimental. Why would anyone want trophies? He shook his head. And then he noticed that his mom's trophy, won at a national finals event, was gone. He hadn't paid much attention over the years, but he didn't want that piece of his history gone.

And why would anyone want it? The only thing he could think was that someone wanted to mess with him, maybe show him they could take what they wanted. They'd made it personal, taking those trophies.

He walked out, left that room, left the barn and headed for the house. Rick didn't follow him. Fortunately no one asked where he was going. He didn't really know.

His gaze settled on the house, a museum of a place in Georgian architecture that his grandfather had built. Columned porticos extended from each side of the house, those massive porches devoid of warmth or furnishings. Rose gardens ran wild because he didn't really care. It was the one thing he'd let go, those flower gardens. They represented his only rebellion against his father's legacy.

Carson took care of business. He took care of the ranch. He maintained the family reputation and standing in the community. He didn't like roses, so if something had to be neglected on a ranch this size it was going to be the flowers.

As he climbed the steps of the front porch a car shot up the driveway, coming to a quick stop in front of the detached garage. He nearly groaned when he saw who it was. His sister, Jenna, five years his junior, and never one to take the family name seriously, jumped out of her little car and reached in the backseat. When she emerged she had her son by the hand. They were both dark haired and dark eyed, and the little boy looked tired.

Jenna looked on the verge of some kind of breakdown.

"Here." She pushed her son's hand into his.

"What?"

"I can't do this. I need a break. Just a few days."

"He isn't a…" Carson looked down at the little guy and bit back every foul word he wanted to say to his sister. Her child wasn't a puppy. He wasn't something you handed off, like secondhand toys or clothing. He was a person with feelings.

And little feet that shifted back and forth as the boy squirmed and looked increasingly more uncomfortable.

"Head for the bathroom, Brandon." Carson opened the door for the five-year-old. The little boy shot past him and into the house.

"He's out of control," Jenna informed Carson. As if that was his fault. He considered telling his sister that her son wasn't out of control. She was.

"I'm not the one dragging him from town to town and from relationship to relationship, Jenna. That's on you. Stay here, be a mom and take care of your son."

"Don't judge me."

He groaned. "Why is it when people are messing up and someone points it out to them, they always fall back on judgment? I'm not judging you. I'm telling you the truth."

"Carson, I just need a few days. I need a break."

"You're a mom, Jenna. I don't think you get to walk away from that."

"I'm not walking away. I just need for you to do this for me. Just this once. I promise when I come back I'll do better. I'll get my act together."

"I think you should definitely get your act together. But stay here and do it. Don't walk away."

Tears were streaming down her face, and Carson took a step toward her. She shook her head.

"Carson, I don't know who I am anymore. I don't know why everything is going wrong and I can't seem to make it right. I can't be the mom Brandon needs. I've never been a good wife. I'm just empty. I have to go."

"No." Carson reached for her hand, but she evaded and headed down the steps.

"I'll be back soon. I promise," she called out as she got in her car.

He would have gone after her, but Brandon came out of the house, wide-eyed and mouth agape. When the little guy looked as if he was about to run after the car, Carson snatched him up.

Together they watched the little red car speed down the driveway.

"So, Brandon, have you had breakfast?" He didn't know what else to say.

Or what else to do. He didn't know what to do with a kid. He didn't know how long it would take his sister to get her head on straight. Days? Weeks?

Brandon sniffled and a few tears slipped down his cheeks. "I spilled the milk last night, and there wasn't anything to eat this morning."

Carson pulled the door open and marched his nephew inside. First things first: food.

As he rummaged around looking for kid-friendly food, he thought about Jenna. His sister had seemed lost for years. Their mom's death had rocked their family, but maybe it had been hardest on a girl just about to enter her teens. When he looked back he realized she'd always drifted. She'd gone from relationship to relationship. She'd never quite found herself. And now Brandon was suffering for it.

He found cereal in the cabinet that hadn't been opened. It looked like the kind full of sugar and obviously what a boy would most want for breakfast. He poured a bowl for Brandon, then poured one for himself.

As soon as he got Brandon settled at the table with breakfast he needed to call in the theft of the trophies. It didn't amount to much, but they needed every theft on record.

He thought about how he would question Ruby Donovan and her brother without really appearing to blame the younger man. Because everyone was a suspect at this point. He wouldn't doubt if some people in town were putting his name on a list.

As he contemplated, something crashed. A shriek followed. He hadn't been watching Brandon. He turned in time to see the curtain rod over the French doors come crashing down. The curtains fell, the picture frames on the wall to the left of the door shattered and glass flew everywhere.

Brandon was in the middle of the mess on an overturned chair.

"What in the world?" Carson lifted the boy out of the mess.

"I was going to try and get that spider." Brandon pointed.

Carson groaned and shook his head. He had to find something to do with a five-year-old until Jenna came to her senses. But first they needed breakfast and a trip to the Donovans'.

* * *

Ruby walked down to the old barn that had been on her family farm since almost the beginning. And it looked every bit of its almost one hundred years. The weathered, wood-sided structure leaned a little from time, from wind and rain, but it was sturdy.

There were a few stalls inside, a hayloft in the top of the barn and a good corral. It was perfect for the business she wanted to start: teaching young children to ride. It wouldn't bring in a lot of money, but until she could buy more livestock to replenish what had been sold off over the past few years and get a job, it would have to do.

Derek joined her, looking over the barn with the same critical eye she'd used moments earlier. He brushed a hand through his dark chestnut hair. The sun captured just the slightest hint of red. He was tall and thin, too thin. He had her hazel eyes but with darker, thicker lashes. He looked like their dad. And it worried her that sometimes he acted like Earl Donovan. Restless. Their dad had always been restless. He'd been a cowboy, a saddle bronc rider and an alcoholic.

"How can I help?" Derek asked. This was the new Derek, the kid who wasn't quite twenty but wanted to change his life. She didn't credit prison with that change; she credited his new-found faith.

People might doubt that faith. She didn't. It was no jailhouse conversion.

"There isn't a lot we can do," she admitted. "I have to get students. So far I have three. That isn't even going to pay the feed bill. I need ten a week. Even that isn't a living."

"We've got a dozen steers we can take to the auction next month. By then they should bring enough to keep us solvent for a little while. And I'm going to get a job at the steakhouse washing dishes."

She closed her eyes at the revelation. "Thank you."

"It's my farm and my family, too. Sometimes you forget that, Ruby. It isn't all on you."

She leaned into his shoulder, and he patted her back before moving away. She smiled, because he'd never enjoyed her displays of sisterly affection. "I'm proud of you, Derek."

"And I'm not going to let you down. I'm almost twenty. It's time for me to get my head on straight and figure some things out."

"Yes, well, I'm nine years older than you and I can say the same about my life."

"You had a career, sis, and you gave it up to come home and help out. You'll get another job."

"You're right. I will. I really hope I can get on with the state. I'm just not sure I want to continue being a caseworker."

He walked with her to the field where a half dozen ponies and small horses grazed on grass that was brown. The animals were all colors, all sizes. But they were gentle and well broke.

"There was another theft last night," Derek said as he leaned against the wood fence. "You know they're going to come here, right?"

"I know."

Four head of cattle from a farm that ran hundreds of head. Why just four? The thieves were being careful? Or maybe unsure of how to dispose of the animals?

From what she'd heard they were hitting farms that had recently purchased animals, so the cattle weren't yet branded. That was smart on their part and meant the thieves knew the ranches.

A truck pulled up to the house. Ruby glanced in that direction and groaned. "Why?"

"Because the guy still has a thing for you?" Derek said with a grin.

"I think that's the furthest thing from the truth." She watched as Carson Thorn got out of his truck, and then she watched as he stood there waiting for something. Or someone.

She saw the someone. A little boy with dark

hair and the same confident swagger as Carson. The two headed her way, discussing something that appeared to be of major importance if the serious look on their faces meant anything. Carson shook his head. The little boy frowned. Carson looked away but not before she saw his lips turn in amusement.

"Carson," she greeted with her best formal tone. All business. That was how she wanted to keep him, in the category of the past, and business.

"Ruby," he said, tipping his hat.

"And this is?" She knelt in front of the child. "That's a great hat."

The miniature Carson pushed his white cowboy hat back and gave her a careful look before nodding in the direction of the horses. "I'm Brandon. Are those your ponies?"

"Yes, they are."

"My mom says I'm about big enough to start riding." His gaze shifted to Derek. "Wow, that belt buckle is cool."

She glanced up and saw the buckle in question. The one their father had won for a national championship. A belt buckle she'd told Derek to get rid of. He could sell it. He could give it away. She didn't care. But she did care that he held on to the past and to his hero worship of their father.

Derek shot her a look telling her to mind her own business.

"Thanks." Derek glanced toward the ponies. "Want to check them out? Carson can list all the reasons why I'm…"

Derek stopped himself with a warning look from Ruby. The last thing they needed was for Derek to antagonize Carson Thorn.

The little boy looked at him, waiting expectantly for him to finish what he planned to say.

"Carson can tell you why I'm the best person to teach you to rope," Derek finished with a grin.

Ruby watched her brother walk away with the child. She looked back at Carson, watched him watching the two—one tall and lanky, the other small and confident. She hated that looking at Carson brought it all back—the hope, the laughter. The dreams.

The heartache.

Smoke and mirrors, she realized now. It had all been an illusion. The smoke cleared and she'd seen reality the day Carson's dad had handed her a check and told her to go to college, be someone, but not to count on being a Thorn.

"Did you put up the cameras?" Carson asked as he continued to watch Derek with the child. They had retrieved a rope from the barn. Derek was showing the little boy how it worked and then letting him give it a shot. The lasso flew through the air and fell to the ground short of the target—the fence post.

"No. I have to wait until I can pay an electrician. And why are you really here? The cattle stolen last night?"

"No."

"Something else?"

"He's my nephew. Jenna's son," Carson said, watching the little boy climb the fence and reach for a buckskin pony the color of wheat.

That wasn't really an answer to her question. She considered pushing, but why? His answer would probably just upset her. Not only that, but she'd latched on to another issue that proved she couldn't be in Little Horn and not get all tangled up in the past.

"Is Jenna in town?" Silly question. If her son was in town, she was in town.

"No," he answered, his firm lips held in a straight and unforgiving line. "She showed up early this morning and dropped him off. I'm not quite sure what to do with him."

"How long do you think you'll have him?"

He rubbed a hand across his jaw and shook his head. "I don't have a clue. She said a few days, but I'm a little worried."

"About her?" She shouldn't care. She shouldn't

delve into his life or the uncertainty in his expression.

"Yes. But I'll call her later and see what we can figure out."

"If she's leaving him for any length of time, he should probably be in school."

His eyes narrowed and he looked down at her. "I hadn't thought that far ahead. She took me by surprise."

"Ambushed." She grinned as she said it.

"Something like that."

"You'll have to enroll him if she doesn't come back."

He nodded but his gaze had drifted back to the boy. "Once I can talk to her and get more out of her than she needs time, I'll do what I have to do. What are the ponies for?"

"Riding lessons."

He nodded yet again and headed that way, toward the horses, her brother, his nephew. She followed.

"Where are the security cameras?" he asked as he stopped to watch Derek lift his nephew over the fence and to the ground.

"In the back of my truck," Ruby answered. "Derek, could you get a saddle for the buckskin?"

Derek let a shoulder rise and fall. "Sure. Brandon, let me lift you back over the fence."

Brandon shook his head. "I can do it."

Sure enough he climbed the fence, dropping to the ground next to his uncle. His very solemn uncle, who watched him as if he was some type of alien creature. She guessed to Carson the child was foreign and strange.

He was a child. Carson had probably never been a child. Even as a teenager he'd been older than his years. She imagined as a boy he'd been just as serious.

"Which saddle?" Derek asked as he headed to the barn.

"I only have three. Grab the one you think will work best."

"What are you doing?" Carson asked.

"Giving your nephew a free riding lesson. And then you can tell everyone what a great time he had."

"Can I?" he asked.

"Please," she added. And he smiled, shifting the seriousness from his features, relaxing just enough to make him look younger, less controlled. More like himself.

"It would be a decent thing to do," Derek added.

"Yes, it would," Carson agreed. His careful gaze lingered on the six horses in varied sizes from pony to small horse.

After a cautious look at the two of them,

Derek walked away, taking his new friend with him. Ruby was left to deal with Carson and leftover emotions that should have been put to rest years ago.

It wouldn't help to look at him, to look into brown eyes that were at once serious and warm. It wouldn't help to think about how it had felt to stand this close to him at seventeen, thinking they would always be together.

What helped was thinking about how it felt to leave thinking he might come after her, that he might still want her once he realized how much she'd given up for him.

He hadn't come looking for her. She'd done her best to forget.

Chapter Three

"Do you have a ladder?" Carson shifted his attention away from the horses, away from watching Derek Donovan as he saddled a small buckskin pony.

Ruby started at the question, her eyes widening. She shook her head and then it must have dawned on her what he'd asked.

"Of course."

"You give Brandon the riding lesson and I'll install your security cameras. I'll wire them in here with the light. Send Derek over to help me."

She chewed on her bottom lip, studying him, thinking, he was sure, about the past. He didn't have time for the past.

"I'm trying to help you out."

"I get that," she answered, still looking unsure. "I know you want to help. I also know you're here to question my brother. So it doesn't make sense to wire cameras if you all think he's the thief. We don't have much to steal, and he isn't going to steal from his own family."

"I just think he ought to be ready to tell people where he was last night."

Her eyes narrowed and she exhaled. Her cheeks flushed pink, and her eyes glittered with anger and unshed tears. "And sometimes I think you're about to be nice. But then you're not. If you must know, we took Gran to the ER."

"I'm sorry." And he meant it. Man, he really meant it. He was sorry he'd asked the question. He was sorry Iva was sick. He was sorry that this woman had taken his dad's money over what he thought they'd shared.

But maybe at nineteen he hadn't really understood what they'd shared. He'd been a kid. She'd been a kid. Maybe his dad had been right; they were rushing into things too young.

"Is Iva okay?" he asked, going for the topic that made sense.

"She's good. They changed her medication and she got a little light-headed."

"I see. You know," he started to offer help, but pulled back the reins on emotions that could get the best of him. "If Derek wants to help, I can show him how to do this, and next time he can take care of it."

She nodded, but she didn't look like someone about to accept his offer. She'd told him years ago it was easier to do it herself than to count on someone and be let down. She'd been young, determined to take care of her family, determined to do something with her life.

Her determination had been everything to him. Because she'd been determined to make him laugh, to make him forget expectations that everyone had for him.

When she nodded, accepting his offer, it took him by surprise.

"The ladder is in the storage room in the barn. I'll get the cameras for you." She started to walk away. He stopped her by reaching for her arm and holding her in one place for that brief moment.

"We're neighbors. You know to call if you need anything."

She pulled free. "Yes, of course."

With that she walked away. He watched her go through the gate, joining Derek and Brandon. The wind blew her hair and she brushed it back. He saw her smile at Brandon, say something that had the kid grinning big. She ruffled his hair and they both laughed.

Derek left her side and headed toward the

barn. Carson walked through the open door. Inside the dim interior he found the ladder, found tools that he'd need, and then Derek was there, watching.

"She's a good person, you know." Derek stood tall, shoulders back. He'd grown since those days when Carson and Ruby had dated. He'd been about seven or so, and he'd wanted to tag along, sharing information about bugs he'd seen and cool cartoons he'd watched.

"I know she is," Carson admitted. "Want to help me out?"

"Sure, I'll help you out. And I'll give you advice. The first time you hurt her, I was a kid. I'm not a kid anymore."

"I get that." Carson carried the ladder past Derek. He got what the other man was saying, but he would like to know how her walking out on him had become his fault.

He didn't plan on having that conversation with her brother. Instead, he set the ladder up against the side of the barn.

"Want to give me a hand?" he asked as he climbed the ladder.

Derek flashed a big grin and pushed back his hat. "Sure. You climb on up and I'll push the ladder over."

"That isn't exactly what I meant. Hand me the first camera and wire nuts. I'm going to…"

Derek started to do just that but both of their gazes landed on the car coming up the drive.

"Great. That's just what we need, more law." Derek looked up at him. "Did you do this?"

"No, Derek, I didn't do this. But you have an alibi, so relax."

Derek shook his head. "From the guy who wants me back behind bars."

"I didn't say that." Carson came down from the ladder and stood next to him as the sheriff pulled up in her patrol car. "There's no evidence you've stolen anything."

"No, there isn't. That's because I haven't. I got in trouble a couple of years ago and I learned my lesson."

"I'm sure you have." Carson wanted to believe Derek. He did seem like a changed person.

Lucy got out of her patrol car, pushing sunglasses back and surveying the property. Derek went forward. Carson followed, but he shot a gaze in Ruby's direction, watching her lead the pony that Brandon rode. She had gone still and even from a distance he felt her silent accusation.

"Lucy," Derek started. "I guess you're here to look for stolen property?"

Carson had to give it to Derek, he wasn't acting guilty.

Lucy pushed back short, blond hair and looked around the place, a frown turning her lips. "Yeah, afraid so. Derek, I'm going to ask you to take a seat in my patrol car. It will make things easier as I take a look around."

Derek slid into the backseat of the car. His jaw clenched, his eyes closed. Carson felt a truckload of sorry for him.

"I haven't seen anything, Lucy." The defense came unplanned but there it was, hanging between them as Ruby walked up, Brandon at her side.

"You haven't seen anything because there's nothing to see. We were at the ER with Gran. You can check it out, pull video, whatever you need to do." Ruby had a hold of Brandon's hand. The boy squirmed and shifted from foot to foot. She gave him a look, her expression softening to tender. "I'm going to take Brandon inside. Gran has some great cookies and chocolate milk. I'll be back."

Carson watched her go. He guessed if he wanted to keep a wall between himself and Ruby Donovan, this was the way to do it. She wouldn't want much to do with him as long as her brother was a prime suspect in the robberies. He could do without the complication of getting involved in her family drama.

It was a win-win situation.

Other than the fact that the guy in the backseat was being accused when there wasn't a bit of evidence against him. This entire situation was getting out of hand. The thefts, people turning against each other. Carson didn't know how they would stop what felt like a train speeding down the track, about to derail.

He didn't know how he would steer clear of Ruby Donovan and whatever still lingered between them.

Ruby stormed through the house, Brandon in tow. The little boy hurried to keep up with her. As she headed into the kitchen, Gran looked up from her seat on the walker that was pushed up to the counter. Frail was something Iva Donovan refused to be. Even after a night in the ER, she was thinking about feeding her family. Her eyes lit on the child Ruby had dragged in with her.

"You trying to pull his arm off, Ruby?"

Ruby stopped, bringing the child to a halt next to her. "No. Oh, Brandon, I'm sorry. Down the hall, buddy. That's the room you're looking for. I'll get your cookies and milk."

"What's going on? And isn't that Jenna's child?"

"Yes, it is Jenna's child. Carson is here. He came over to, I don't know, maybe search the place. Maybe to help put up cameras. I'm not sure. And now Lucy is here because there was another theft last night."

She poured milk and opened the cookie jar. Brandon came back down the hall. He climbed up on a stool and waited.

"Someone took Uncle Carson's trophies that were his mom's," the child said as he reached for a cookie. His elbow hit the milk and it tumbled, sending liquid spilling across the counter. "Oops."

Ruby reached for a roll of paper towels and wiped up the mess. "Oops. The nice thing about messes is that they clean up."

"Yeah, my mom says I'm clumsy and she's tired of cleaning up after me. I make a lot of messes."

"Kids do, Brandon." Ruby shoved off the caseworker ingrained deep within. She no longer had that job. She was here restoring a farm, finding a way to get back to the life she had walked out on years ago.

She'd moved to Oklahoma after college. She'd visited when she could. She'd sent money home to help her grandmother who insisted on keeping the farm.

"Where is Carson?" Iva asked as she peeled carrots.

"Outside with Derek and Lucy. I'm sure they're going through the barn."

"Looking for trophies," Brandon supplied as he munched down on a cookie.

"Oh, yes, trophies." Ruby drew in a breath. "I'm going to check on the pony. He needs to be unsaddled. Brandon, you stay here with my granny and I'll be back."

Brandon grinned. "Because Uncle Carson needs someone to take him down a notch. That's what my mom always says."

Iva snickered and tossed a half carrot to the child. "Eat something good for you, little man. If your mouth is full it won't run quite so much. And Ruby, head on out of here before you blow a gasket."

Ruby took her grandmother's advice and headed for the front door, barely noticing the worn furniture, the threadbare rugs and the dust. There was so much to do. She didn't know when she'd get it all done. The house, the farm, even Derek and Iva were in need of her attention.

As was the bank account that was dwindling to an all-time low.

As she walked down the steps she saw Carson heading her way. Derek walked with him. The two were talking in a way that settled her nerves, because the conversation seemed halfway civil. She waited until they got to her and then she nodded toward the house, sending Derek on his way.

He paused, looking down at her, a reminder that he was no longer a little boy needing her protection. He was a grown man. He could take care of himself.

She had to let go.

But she couldn't.

Derek started to say something, shook his head and went on inside. That left Ruby facing Carson. She lifted her head, determined to give him a verbal thrashing, but when their gazes clashed, she couldn't. The words froze and time faded. She was seventeen again, telling him goodbye as he went off to college. She wasn't strong or brave. She wasn't able to hold it all together.

That girl was long gone. She took a deep breath and let her gaze drift from his to the few cattle in their field grazing down the grass that wouldn't get them through the winter.

"He didn't take the trophies. Why would he do that?"

Carson drew back at the question. "I didn't…"

She held up her hand. "You can't talk around a child. They have a tendency to not keep secrets."

He rubbed a hand over his brow and nodded. "You're right. And I'm sorry."

"Are you? Sorry, that is? After all, you appear to think you're in the right. You brought that little boy over pretending you were going to help out, be neighborly, but what you wanted to do is snoop. And then Lucy showed up. Is that all coincidence?"

"Actually, it is a coincidence that she showed up. But I will admit I did come over to look…" He sighed and even looked a little ashamed.

Good.

"Of course you did. And now that you have seen, you can go."

He didn't move. She waited, arms crossed, trying her best to appear brave as she faced him down. She arched an eyebrow for good measure.

Impatient, he jerked off his cowboy hat and brushed a hand through his hair. "Ruby, can we call a truce?"

"Why?"

"Because we're neighbors. Because we used to be friends."

She arched an eyebrow once again.

He cleared his throat and jammed his hat down on his head. "Fine, we were more than friends."

Would a third eyebrow arch be too much? She sighed. "Yes, we were more than friends.

But then it was made known to me that I wasn't quite good enough."

"You were good enough." He said it quietly. "More than good enough."

"Okay, well, let's not go there, because we have different versions of the story."

"I guess we do. Someday we'll have to compare notes."

She shook her head. "No, I'd rather not. I have a reason for being here, and you're not included in that. I'm here for my grandmother and brother. I'm here to get this little ranch back in the black. Now, if you'll excuse me."

"I have to get Brandon," he reminded her with an amused glint in his eyes.

"Of course you do." So much for a dramatic exit. "I'll get him for you."

"Hey, Ruby, I'd like to enroll him in your riding class. And maybe Derek could teach him to rope."

She had made it to the steps of the house and his words stopped her. Of all the things he could have said, she wished it hadn't been that. Not him on this ranch, in her life, in her thoughts. Her heart still ached remembering how it had felt to know he was no longer a part of her world. She couldn't let him back in knowing how that heartbreak had felt.

But she couldn't turn down the money one more student would bring.

She turned, eyed the rancher standing in her yard, out of place in those poor surroundings. She'd been just as out of place in his world. They'd had a different circle of friends in high school. They'd had different experiences. Their worlds had clashed.

His dad had been right, telling her they would understand when they got older and were thinking with brains and not hormones.

"Have him here Monday afternoon at four. And don't forget to enroll him in school."

He inclined his head. "Sure thing. Thank you."

"I'll get him for you."

She headed up the steps, leaving Carson in the yard. But she didn't make it inside. Gran opened the door, Brandon right behind her.

"Carson, this is a fine little man you've got." Iva eased her walker out the door, and Brandon followed. Ruby held the door for her grandmother and she avoided looking at Carson.

"Thank you, Iva. I hope he was good."

"Of course he was good," Iva assured him. "And he hasn't been to church. A child shouldn't be raised without some grounding in the word."

At that, Carson chuckled, the sound low and

vibrating against Ruby's nerves, already strung tight from his presence. "Iva, you think you've finally found a way to force my hand."

Ruby let the door close as her grandmother stepped out of the way. Iva sat down on the seat of her walker. "Of course I have. When you come to church, you all can come over here for lunch after. I'll make apple pie."

"Gran," Ruby started.

Iva cut her off. "I'm being neighborly, Ruby Jo. Brandon needs church and it wouldn't hurt Carson to have something sweet in his life."

Ruby wanted the porch to open up and swallow her. Instead, she gave Carson a meaningful glare, daring him to accept the offer.

He ignored her, his focus 100 percent on her grandmother.

"I'd love to come over, Iva. It might not be this weekend, but soon."

Iva cackled because she'd won. "That sounds good. It will be nice to have a big family lunch."

"Family dinners and apple pie are always a good bribe and you know it." He leaned to kiss Iva's cheek. Ruby rolled her eyes. He was that good. Just waltz in, charm her grandmother and invade her life.

And she'd get the lecture once he left because she was only Ruby Jo when she was in trouble.

He left, taking Brandon by the hand and

leading the little boy across the lawn to his big Ford truck. Ruby waited until the truck was heading down the drive before she allowed herself to look at her grandmother.

"Why?"

Iva looked innocent, her eyebrows drawing in over narrowed eyes. "What?"

"You know what. You invited Carson to lunch. Seriously? It's bad enough that he wants me to give his nephew riding lessons, but having him here for lunch is too much."

Iva gave her a long, steady look. "Only if you are still bothered by his presence. If he doesn't mean anything to you, why would it be a problem to have him around?"

"Because he thinks my brother is a thief. Because his family discarded me like trash. Because…"

Iva did the eyebrow arch this time. Ruby didn't want to see how much she resembled her grandmother in that gesture.

"I know they hurt you. But I also know that you and Carson never talked about all of that. The check. His sister. It's all in the past, but it's also been buried and has been festering for a dozen years. Neither of you has moved on. Neither of you has gotten over being mad at the other."

"I think we have moved on. I got a job in Oklahoma. He's running the family ranch."

"Yes, you've moved on. But it's like running in place. Neither of you has gotten anywhere."

"Gran…"

Her grandmother pushed herself to her feet. "Oh, Ruby, stop worrying. It's just lunch and it might not happen for weeks. Or ever."

"Yes, just lunch." With a man she'd once loved. A man she'd thought she would marry.

A man who was still kind and caring. She knew he'd helped her grandmother. Now she knew he was willing to care for a nephew. She knew he cared about his community.

She wanted to paint him as the villain, but she couldn't. She knew him. And knowing him made him even more dangerous.

Chapter Four

❧

On Saturday morning Carson headed to town with Brandon in tow. And Brandon in tow was easier said than done. Even though it was only nine in the morning he'd already done a good day's work. With his nephew tagging along, it had been double duty. Especially when by eight the kid in question had managed to open a gate and let out a few horses. He'd caught the wild barn cat and managed to get scratched up good. And then he'd turned on the water in the bathroom and left it running.

As he drove Carson tossed his hat on the truck seat and brushed a hand through his hair. He cast a sideways look at the little boy and shook his head. The kid was almost asleep. And sleeping he looked pretty innocent. Cute, even. Carson felt the corner of his mouth tug up. Yeah, he wasn't a bad kid. He just hadn't had a lot of structure with Jenna.

This morning he'd asked Carson when his mommy was coming back. Carson shook his head at that, because he didn't have an answer. He'd even tried to call his sister. She hadn't answered.

Carson pulled up to Maggie's Coffee Shop, grinning because not too long ago someone had stopped in town thinking to find one of those fancy city coffee places, not realizing a coffee shop was a diner with biscuits and gravy, strong coffee in a mug and maybe chicken fried steak for a lunch special.

"Ready for breakfast?" he asked his half-asleep nephew.

Brandon perked up. "Yeah. Pancakes, please!"

"You got it."

He got out of the truck and motioned Brandon across, to get out on his side. The boy grabbed his own white cowboy hat and, with a grin, pushed it down on his head. He looked up at Carson, happy again and wide-awake. Together they walked up the sidewalk to Maggie's. The place was packed, as he'd expected on a Saturday morning. Town was packed. He'd seen a dozen cars at Big Jim's grocery store, and a half-dozen cars lined up at the pumps of the gas station. He guessed it was the nice weather. People wanted to get out and enjoy weather that was cool after a summer that had felt like they lived in a furnace.

He knew what to expect when he walked through the door of Maggie's. A couple dozen men would be drinking coffee and solving the world's problems. And a few would be trying to solve the thefts that had been hitting their community.

"Hey, Carson," Ben Stillwater from the Stillwater ranch called out and motioned to an empty chair at their table.

A table with Byron McKay and his twin boys, Winston and Gareth. The boys were sixteen and fortunately didn't look much like their dad. They both had strawberry blond hair like him but favored their momma otherwise, and they had that look of too much money and not enough responsibility.

Ben Stillwater was a twin, too. His identical twin, Grady, was in the army and stationed in Afghanistan. Ben had stayed home to rodeo and continue running the Stillwater ranch. They were identical, but that didn't mean they were exactly alike.

"Who do you have with you?" Ben asked, reaching for a chair at a nearby table and placing it next to him. "Is this Jenna's almost grown son?"

Brandon grinned and took the seat next to Ben. "I'm five."

"I reckon you are." Ben shot Carson a questioning look that he could only answer with a shrug of a shoulder.

Carson took the other empty chair and turned over the coffee cup sitting in front of him. The waitress, Sally Ann, only worked Saturdays. She smiled at the two of them as she hurried their way with coffee and menus.

"What are you all having today, Carson?"

"I'll take the Saturday-morning special and Brandon would like pancakes and bacon. And to drink he'll take—"

"Chocolate milk," Brandon shouted.

Next to Carson, Ben laughed. "He's going to keep you on your toes, my friend."

"Yeah, I guess he will."

Brandon gave Carson a look and then he turned to Ben. "I don't think he can get on his toes. And Ruby is going to take him down a notch."

Ben laughed loud and long. People turned to stare. Carson shot him a look, hoping to quell his mirth.

"That's about the best thing I've heard in a long time." Ben held his hand up. "Give me a fiver, little man."

Brandon grinned and slapped his palm

against Ben's. Carson turned away from the two, hoping that would keep Ben from asking questions about Ruby and how Brandon would have heard her say anything about him.

The conversation across the table between Byron and another rancher caught Carson's attention. He sipped his coffee and listened to the coffee shop gossip.

The foreman for the Marley ranch, a spread on the other side of town, came in and sat at the table next to theirs.

"Is it true you all got hit last night?" Byron asked as he shoveled a big bite of eggs into his mouth.

"Yeah, ten head and they burned a few bales of hay. That's leading me to believe we don't have professional cattle thieves on our hands. Professionals don't light up a blaze to let everyone know they're around."

"Professionals don't keep hitting small and taking things that don't really matter," Ben interjected as he cut up his biscuits and gravy.

The waitress showed up with Carson and Brandon's food. She refilled his coffee, placed the bill next to his plate and took a second to talk to the little boy in their midst. He was eyeing pancakes heaped with butter, chocolate chips and syrup.

"Byron, have you all seen Betsy since her

daddy died?" Ben asked, always being the one willing to wade right into troubled waters.

Brandon, only five but not oblivious to tension, looked up, watching the men at the table. Carson sighed, wishing Ben had left well enough alone. Byron and his cousin Mac McKay had never been close. Mac had run his small farm, but that hadn't been enough to pay the bills. And when it all had come crashing in, when he'd needed the help of a relative, Byron had turned him down flat.

No one wanted to dwell on the night Mac, in a drunken stupor, had walked in front of a car. Betsy, his only child, had left town. Eighteen and on her own. Carson liked to think there were folks in town, himself included, who would have helped her out had she stayed. He only wished Mac would have taken his offer of help.

"Betsy isn't my problem," Byron blustered. That brought Carson back to the conversation. "The girl is just like her dad. She isn't going to get anything out of life if she isn't willing to work for it. I didn't give Mac handouts and I won't give her any."

"She's a kid," Winston McKay spoke softly from his chair just a few seats down the table. He glanced at his dad and went back to eating.

The two boys looked at each other. Meaningful looks. Carson watched, interested, and his opinion of the two boys came up a notch.

Byron didn't seem to share his opinion. "If I find out you two have been helping her, you will find out what it's like to not have anything."

Ben cleared his throat. "Let's take it down a notch. We've got a little cowboy here trying to eat his breakfast. And I'd like to enjoy mine."

"Agreed," Carson voiced his opinion to let things settle a little.

Byron blustered and set his cup down, slopping coffee on the bill next to his plate. He brushed it off with a napkin.

"Yesterday Lucy went out to the Donovan place again," Byron said, changing the subject without much finesse. "I still say that kid is guilty and we ought to just arrest him."

Carson sat back, looking at the other man and wondering why he couldn't just be reasonable. "Byron, there are a few problems with that thought. Number one, 'we' can't arrest anyone. Number two, the kid doesn't have any of the stolen property. You can't arrest someone just because you don't like them."

"And you're only taking up for him because that sister of his is back in town, and you've forgotten that your daddy didn't want you messing around—"

"Be quiet." Carson leaned across the table. "I've had enough, Byron. You want to accuse your neighbors, stir up trouble and pit people against each other. But as far as I know the Donovans have never done a thing to you."

"I'm just saying they aren't any better than that cousin of mine was. Mac wanted my money, my resources. They'll take what they can—"

Carson raised a hand. He didn't need to hear any more. He was sure his dad had probably told Byron about the payoff to Ruby. That didn't mean the rest of the county needed to hear it.

"Byron, the last thing I need today is a case of indigestion, so let's leave off. We can talk about something that matters or enjoy a little peace and quiet."

Ben cleared his throat. "I hear she's giving riding lessons. I sold her a pony a few weeks ago. She's going to need saddles if anyone has old ones they aren't using."

Carson started to answer but before he could get the words out, Byron scooted his chair back and stood. He gave his boys a meaningful glare.

"I guess I'll just leave," Byron grumbled as he grabbed the bill next to his plate. "But I want you to know, as vice president of the league, I'm going to start organizing patrols. Call it a neighborhood watch if that makes you and Lucy happy. If our sheriff can't solve these crimes, we'll do it ourselves."

"Go ahead, Byron. I'm not going to stop you."

His boys stood up, a nod acknowledging the other men at the table as they followed their dad out. Ben whistled and leaned his chair back on two legs.

"That man is strung tighter than his fences!"

"Yeah, just a little."

"About Ruby," Ben waded in again, a big grin on his face.

"Leave it. Can't a man just eat his breakfast?"

Ben laughed at that. "Yeah, I guess he can."

Carson finished his breakfast, wishing for once that he'd gone out of town for the meal rather than into Maggie's and what appeared to be a real hornet's nest. What he wouldn't give for a quiet life.

Instead of that quiet life he walked out of the diner some thirty minutes later with Brandon in tow. His nephew had managed to knock over his glass of chocolate milk, not once but twice. He'd poured salt in Ben's coffee when they hadn't been looking and he'd unscrewed the lid on the ketchup. Carson had fortunately caught that little trick.

He wasn't so sure Ben hadn't given him the idea to try the trick.

As they walked out the front door, the old adage about things had nowhere to go but up seemed as far off as the moon. Ruby pulled her old farm truck into an empty parking space and hopped out. She saw him and frowned.

Ruby could have gone a whole year without seeing Carson again. Or so she wanted to believe. But she couldn't lie, not even to herself. Seeing him standing on that sidewalk with his nephew almost tore her heart out. It was a reaction she hadn't expected. But seeing him with that little boy took her back. The sight made her think of dreams and what she might have had.

If wishes were ponies, Granny Iva always said. Wishes weren't ponies. Ponies, saddles, bridles and feed were bought with cold, hard cash. Just like Carson's dad had tried to buy her. He'd tried to buy her and he'd tried to threaten her, with Iva as his target. She shook her head to clear that memory.

"Hey, Ruby!" Brandon pulled away from his uncle. "Did you get that new pony you were telling me about?"

"As a matter of fact, I did. Derek hauled him home today."

"Is he fast?"

She smiled, because to a little boy it was all about speed.

"I think he might be the fastest pony I have on the place!"

He started to bounce. She smoothed a hand down the little boy's shoulder.

"What did you have for breakfast?"

"Pancakes with chocolate chips and syrup. And I had bacon. And chocolate milk."

She glanced from the boy to Carson. He shrugged and she shook her head.

"That's a lot of sugar for one little boy," she said, more for Carson than the child. "Maybe tomorrow just have eggs and toast?"

He wrinkled his Thorn nose at her. "I don't like eggs."

"No, I don't imagine you do." She glanced toward Maggie's and then let her gaze settle on Carson. What a mistake. He stood there, relaxed and in control, his keys in his hand. The other hand reached for Brandon. "Is Doc Grainger inside? I called out to the ranch but they said he was in town having coffee."

Doc, as they all called him, had been born and raised on the Grainger spread. As much as the ranch was a part of him, he'd shared that he never felt like a rancher. He was giving the community a year and then he was heading for the city to practice medicine. She, like many others, hoped he'd stay in town.

Ruby knew him well enough to doubt he would.

"Yeah, I think he was sitting in a booth at the back. Is everything okay?" Concern edged into Carson's tone, genuine concern. It softened the brittle tone and softened Ruby's heart a smidge.

"I think everything is okay. Iva doesn't tell me everything, you know. She's tough like that. But this morning I can tell she doesn't feel well, maybe just a cold coming on, but I thought I'd see if he'd stop by the house later. I know he's a pediatrician, but he's always been so good about checking on her."

"If you need anything…"

"We're fine, Carson." Her words didn't sound as strong as she had intended but repeating them in a firmer tone wouldn't serve her purpose, either.

"Can I come by and see the pony? Does he have a name?" Brandon tugged at her hand as he asked the questions.

"His name is Peanut and I will let you ride him Monday when you have your lesson."

Carson stepped closer, Brandon's hand still

in his. "Are you sure everything is okay with Iva? Do you need to drive her to Austin?"

She shook her head. She didn't need his help. She didn't need him close. She didn't need to get all tangled up in leftover emotions. That's all this was, leftovers. They might sound good, but rarely were as good as the first time around. She swallowed and met his warm gaze and saw concern. Inwardly, she cringed. She didn't want his concern. Remembering him as a person who genuinely cared complicated things.

"I'm sure she's fine. But I'll feel better if Doc can come out and check on her."

"Let me know if anything changes. And if you need to cancel on Monday, we'll understand."

At his mention of canceling, Brandon groaned. Ruby smiled down at the little guy. "Don't worry, we won't cancel."

"We'll go then. Let me know if you need anything." Carson walked away with his nephew.

She watched them go, drawn to the pair, drawn by the past and by the present. That was even more of a complication. One she didn't need. It seemed that somewhere beneath the hard exterior, the Carson she knew still lived and breathed.

The door to Maggie's opened and the man

she had been looking for stepped out. Tyler Grainger, tall and all blond good looks, stopped to look around as he pulled car keys out of his pocket. He saw Ruby and nodded.

"Ruby, how's Iva?" Tyler headed her way with an easy gait, comfortable in his own skin. He still looked like a kid who'd grown up in this small town. But she understood wanting to shed that skin and be someone or something else.

"She's not good, Tyler. I'm worried, and of course she refuses to go to the doctor. She says she went and going wears her out."

"I can stop by," he offered as he glanced at the watch on his wrist. "In an hour?"

"If it wouldn't be too much trouble. I know house calls are a thing of the past and this isn't your specialty."

He shrugged off her comments. "I don't mind."

"Thank you."

A truck started. She turned, knowing it would be Carson's and realizing immediately that she shouldn't have turned. It was too easy, this getting pulled into the past, into remembering how he'd cared.

She didn't need those reminders. She didn't need to think about confiding in him the way she once had. No, she had to think about her small family and how to keep them together and keep them solvent.

"Everything okay between you and Carson?" Tyler asked.

"Yes, just fine. I'm just tired. I need to head home and check on Gran. If something comes up and you can't come out, I understand."

"I don't foresee anything coming up. And you know to call me or call 911 if her condition worsens."

"Yes, of course. I don't think it's dire. I'm just not used to seeing her so weak and tired."

"No, you aren't. And Ruby, it's unfortunately going to get worse."

"I wish that wasn't the case."

Tyler's features softened and for a minute he lost that composure that schooled his mouth into an even line. Not a smile. Not a frown. "I wish it wasn't the case, too. But she is going to get worse. Probably sooner and not later. The two of you, or the three of you, should talk about what she wants. I wouldn't wait on that."

"I won't put it off."

She left then, going back to her truck—dazed, afraid and alone. As she backed out of the parking space she saw Carson's truck driving away and she wondered how it would feel to confide her fears in him the way she had once upon a time.

Too many years had passed since she'd been able to turn to him, trust him. It wouldn't do to look back, she told herself as she shifted the truck into gear. She didn't want to remember resting her head on his shoulder and telling him how it had felt when her dad had sold everything, bought a camper and hauled them all over the western US to rodeos. Always chasing that buckle she'd seen on Derek's belt the previous day. He'd finally won it. Only to die a week later in a freak accident in a chute as he settled on the back of a rangy, unknown horse.

The memories evaporated as she drove past the gas station. Her attention was drawn to a cherry-red convertible at the pumps. A young woman stood next to the car, laughing as she spoke to the man standing next to her.

Derek.

Ruby slowed but she didn't stop. Her heart raced, and so did her mind as she thought of all the reasons her brother might be in town and with a young woman obviously not from around here.

"No, Derek. Don't be in on all of this." Ruby spoke to herself in the interior of the rattling old truck.

Of course her brother wasn't in on the thefts. She had to believe in him. He'd paid for his previous crimes. He was going to church and helping her at the ranch. He had goals, and he was slowly letting go of the desire to be their father.

It had taken her years to convince Derek that their dad had been wonderful, but he hadn't made the right choices for his children. After their mother's death he should have brought them here, not packed up and taken off after that crazy dream.

The buckle Derek cherished was a reminder of those chaotic years, struggling to get by with Ruby trying to take care of her father and little brother. What Derek cherished, she wanted to forget.

She shook it off. She didn't have time for melancholy, for memories. She didn't have time to dwell on what could have been or dark-haired little boys who walked next to Carson, mimicking his long strides.

Today she had to think about how to keep a ranch afloat, her brother out of trouble and her grandmother in the best health possible for as long as possible. As she drove past the entrance of the Thorn ranch, she let out a sigh. Some things were easier said than done.

Forgetting Carson was one of those things.

Chapter Five

After a rainy morning, Monday afternoon cleared up. The sun came out. Carson had a list of things to get done. A long list. Instead of checking off a few things on that list, he'd been to the school to register Brandon for kindergarten. The boy would be starting the next day. Now the two of them were on their way to the Donovans' for a riding lesson.

"I'm going to need crayons. And pencils. Even a backpack." Brandon proudly recited the list of things the teacher had told them he would need. Carson let out a sigh that had more to do with not knowing the next step than anything else. Brandon looked at him, his mouth turning down at the corners and his eyes narrowing. "I'm a lot of work."

"What?" Carson jerked himself out of his list making.

"I know that sigh. That's the one my mom uses when I'm a lot of work."

"You're not a lot of work. You're a normal kid and you need things. That's what kids do, Brandon. And it's okay."

Brandon bit down on his lip and studied Carson. "Yeah, okay. But you don't have to get all of that stuff on the list if it's too much trouble."

"It isn't too much trouble." He smiled, amazed by the kid and how easily he let go of what he wanted. As if he was used to not asking for more.

That thought made Carson mad at his sister.

"Okay, but if you change your mind." Brandon turned to look out the window. "Are you sure riding lessons are okay? Derek said he'd teach me to rope."

"Riding lessons are fine, too."

He turned at the entrance and headed up the drive, pulling past the house to the barn and parked. Ruby walked out the side door. Her auburn hair was covered with a white cowboy hat, leaving her face in shadows. But he saw her quick look, saw her lips turn ever so slightly.

Brandon had his seat belt unbuckled and he was reaching for the door. Carson let him go, and he got out a little slower, taking his time. He needed time. He needed to figure out how this woman could crash back into his life this way after the way she'd walked out on him, and it didn't feel as though she'd walked away. It felt like being eighteen again and still believing she was the one.

She wasn't, though. She wasn't the girl he'd thought he loved. She wasn't the person he'd spend his life with. Instead, she was the person who'd taken a check and walked away without a goodbye or an explanation.

That memory alone should have him angry. It should make him question why in the world he was here with Brandon. Why couldn't he let it go?

"Uncle Carson, look at this pony!" Brandon yelled from the fence where he stood next to Ruby. "Isn't he great? And I get to ride him."

"He is a good-looking horse, Brandon." Carson stopped at the fence, placing his hand on his nephew's shoulder. "Let's not yell, though. That's not the best way to act around livestock."

"Oh," Brandon said in a quieter tone. "You're right. But he's so tame he doesn't seem to mind."

"Maybe not, but another horse might."

Ruby led them away from the fence. "Let's get him saddled up. Derek is inside. He's going to help you learn to put a bridle and saddle on

Peanut. And then we'll work him in the corral here."

"But I get to ride him today, right?" Brandon headed into the barn, glancing back just briefly.

"Ride him, yes."

"And I can see how fast he can run," the boy called from inside the barn.

"No, we won't be seeing how fast he runs." Carson entered the barn and saw Brandon watching Derek clean out a stall.

"Soon?" Brandon asked.

"Not until Ruby says you're ready," Carson answered in the firmest tone he could.

Brandon frowned but he didn't argue. Instead, he took the lead rope Derek handed him and followed the other man out a door to the corral. Carson watched from inside the barn as Derek showed the little boy how to approach the horse, helping him clip the lead to the halter, and then the two walked back to the barn, the pony walking next to them.

"He's good with kids, Carson." Ruby defended her brother in tone that told him to agree, not argue.

"Yes, he is."

"People do change," she continued. "He has changed. He isn't stealing from our neighbors.

I would know. If he wasn't here for long periods of time, I'd notice."

He nodded, unsure if she was trying to convince him or herself. As a man with a sister who seemed to be making a lot of mistakes and not changing, he wasn't going to discourage her from believing in her brother.

"People change," he agreed. He had certainly changed from the teenager who'd believed this woman could change everything for him.

It seemed a little nonsensical now to think of her as his sunshine. He'd been the kid with everything. He'd never worried about the next meal, what he'd wear or where he'd live. Those had been her fears. But he'd been the one needing her. He'd needed her warmth, her laughter. He'd needed her because a lost football game hadn't been the end of the world when she'd been at his side. His dad's severe demeanor had been easier to handle when he'd known he could spend time with Ruby.

James Thorn had insisted on perfection and on children who understood the importance of success. Ruby had been a distraction, he'd informed Carson. And he'd taken care of that distraction.

And she'd taken the check his father had offered.

He shouldn't blame her. If his dad hadn't

used money to rid the Thorns of Ruby Donovan, he would have used other means.

"Carson?"

He cleared his throat, swallowing past regret. "Yeah?"

"Are you okay?"

"I'm good," he answered, stepping back as Derek and Brandon entered the barn with the pony. The little bay had a deep red coat, a long black tail and a mane buzzed short.

He watched as they tied the pony, and then Derek showed Carson's nephew how to brush the animal. Carson got hit with more regrets. He should have been the one teaching his nephew these things. Unfortunately, Jenna had steered clear of the family ranch and Carson. She'd lived in Austin, in San Antonio and Dallas. And Brandon had been dragged along.

He would get a lawyer. Somehow he'd keep the boy here, keep Jenna from uprooting him again. There was no reason for a kid to live the way Jenna had her son living.

"Try to smile—you're going to scare the boy." Ruby nudged him, reminding him that he wasn't alone.

"Sorry."

"Don't be. You care about him. That isn't something to apologize for."

He didn't answer. But her shoulder still

leaned into his arm and it made him want to wrap an arm around her and draw her close to his side. He drew in a breath and put some distance between them. She looked up, her eyes narrowing, asking questions.

"Iva's okay today?" he asked, sounding a little abrupt to his own ears.

"Yes, she's better. Tyler said she might have had too much sugar yesterday. She isn't going to change that. She said she's not going to get any better, and eating less sugar won't change that. She likes pecan pie and she'll eat pecan pie." Ruby smiled as she said it, sounding a lot like her grandmother.

Carson chuckled, because he knew Iva and knew she would dig her heels in on anything that didn't make sense to her.

"Did she remind him that she'd changed his diapers more than once and doctored him when he had a cold?"

"Doesn't she use that on anyone who tries to tell her what to do?" Ruby asked, her voice sweet. He got lost in that voice, remembering. Always remembering.

"Yeah, she does." He took a deep breath and got himself back on track. "Derek and Brandon are outside. I think I'll head on out that way."

"Chicken," she called out to his retreating back.

Yeah, he was. But he couldn't help the grin

that latched on as she followed him out the door of the barn.

He'd missed her. He wouldn't deny that because he'd never been one to lie. Not even to himself.

Twelve years of missing someone was a long time. Too bad mistrust was layered in with the missing.

Ruby enjoyed Carson's nephew. The little boy had too much energy and a penchant for trouble, but he also gave good hugs and loved the little pony he'd been riding. As they finished their lesson she let her gaze drift toward the house where Carson had retreated when he'd left the barn.

She could imagine him on the front porch with Iva, telling her stories about town or discussing the thefts. Hopefully he would reassure her that it wasn't Derek, rather than worrying her with concerns that it might be her grandson.

"Can I ride some more?" Brandon asked from the saddle.

"Sorry, kiddo. It's time to let this little guy head back to the field and his friends. But first we'll take care of him. Because taking care of our horses is important, right?"

"Yeah, we'll brush him and feed him. Isn't

that right, Derek?" Brandon waved from the back of the horse.

Ruby smiled at her brother, who stood at the entrance of the barn, waiting. He was on his phone and a big smile spread across his too handsome face. He'd always been cute, her brother. And charming. She dreaded asking about the girl with the convertible. Maybe she wouldn't. Not for a while.

Derek ended the call. "I just saw Eva Brooks coming up the drive, sis. Let me help Brandon take care of Peanut and you head on up and see what she needs."

"Thank you." Ruby watched as Brandon made a big attempt to dismount. Probably the way he'd seen his uncle, with a wide swoop of his right leg and then dropping to the ground on the left side. "Good job, Brandon."

The little boy beamed. "I can't wait to show Uncle Carson."

"He'll be proud. Now you help unsaddle and brush Peanut down. I'll see you at the house."

She left the two and headed down the path toward the house. Eva, already out of her car, headed for the front door with a couple of baskets. She nodded when Ruby waved.

"Hey, Eva. What brings you out this way?"

Eva lifted the two baskets. A cousin to the Stillwaters, Ben and Grady, she lived at their ranch, and Ruby had heard she was trying her hand in the kitchen.

"I brought dinner. We heard Iva wasn't feeling well and thought this might help out."

Ruby took the basket Eva offered. "Thank you so much."

Eva, pretty with fair skin and red hair, blushed and closed her eyes briefly. "Don't thank me until you've tried it. Fortunately, our cook did most of the work. My only contribution was the sweet potatoes."

"I'm sure it's wonderful," Ruby assured the other woman.

Eva wrinkled her nose. "Don't be so sure of that, Ruby. I'm just not sure what to do with myself. It seems like I'm always trying to find where I fit and what I'm good at."

Ruby got that. Maybe she knew what she was good at, but she'd never known where she fit. "Maybe stop trying so hard. What you're good at is what comes natural."

"Thank you. I'm just a little out of sorts right now. I know I'll figure something out, and Ben has been great to let me stay at the ranch," Eva paused. "How is Iva feeling?"

"She's good. Come on up to the house and see for yourself."

Ruby led the way up the worn path to the front porch of the house. Iva stepped out, followed by Carson, who reached past her to hold the door so she could maneuver her walker. When Iva saw Eva, her eyes lit up.

"Well, Eva Brooks, what a sight for sore eyes. You haven't visited in forever."

"I've been busy at the ranch, Iva. But we wanted to bring you all dinner."

Iva motioned the younger woman up and Eva went, taking the hug Iva gave her. Ruby smiled at the display. Everyone from forty years old and down was a kid Iva knew, had helped take care of or taught in Sunday school. She had deep roots in this community.

"This is wonderful," Iva said, letting go of Eva. "Carson, you and Brandon should stay and eat with us. Eva, you, too."

Eva had stepped off the porch, her keys already in hand. "No, I'm going to help do the dishes back at the house. But you all enjoy. I'll stop back by and get the baskets in a day or two."

"I can bring them over," Ruby offered.

"Either way." Eva waved as she headed for her car. "Enjoy your dinner."

Not a chance of that, Ruby thought. Not with Brandon already back from the barn and cheering the idea of staying for dinner, and Carson telling Iva that would be great. Ruby's safe world felt invaded by Thorns. Her heart felt invaded.

There was nothing to do but face it. She smiled big, as if it was all a great idea, and she handed the baskets to Derek, who took them inside. Carson held the door for Iva and Ruby waited on the porch, taking in fresh air and clearing her head. Brandon looked up at her, his grin splitting his young face.

"Are you mad?" he asked.

Ruby shook her head. "No, of course not. Why do you ask that, Brandon?"

"My mom always takes deep breaths when she says, 'Brandon, you've gone too far.'"

Poor kid. It sounded as if his momma had a hard time with his energetic little self. Ruby brushed a hand through his dark hair and shook her head. "I'm not mad."

"Okay," he said, biting down on his bottom lip. "Not even at me?"

"Definitely not at you."

He seemed okay with that answer and he reached for her hand, walking inside with her. Not for the first time Ruby saw this little house through the eyes of Carson Thorn. She saw the worn furniture, the paneled walls, the dim lighting. She saw it, and she didn't care. This was her home. It was her safe place. And she loved it for all its worn, outdated fixtures.

She loved the table in the kitchen, scarred but smooth pine that her grandfather had made by hand fifty years ago. She loved the way the kitchen always smelled as if something good was in the oven. And usually was.

Derek had placed the baskets on the counter and was pulling out the dishes. "Fried chicken, mashed potatoes and gravy, rolls, sweet potatoes and a chocolate cream pie."

"Sounds lovely. I can't remember the last time a neighbor brought me a meal." Iva leaned in to look at the bounty.

Ruby stepped behind her grandmother and gave her a hug. "That is because you are always the one bringing the dishes. Now go sit and we'll get this on the table."

"There's fresh sun tea in the fridge," Iva said as she moved away. "Brandon, you come sit with me and tell me all about your riding lesson."

Ruby watched her grandmother make her way slowly to the table. Her heart clenched with fear at the sight. Because Gran was slowing down. They would have to talk about the future. A hand, strong and firm, settled on her back. She closed her eyes at the comfort in that touch.

"It's okay." He spoke close to her ear.

She nodded, wanting to agree, but a tear

squeezed past her closed eyes. She swiped it away, took a deep breath and opened her eyes to turn and smile up at him. Of course it was okay.

"Thank you," she whispered.

But he was already moving away from her, away from the contact that she'd needed so desperately. She wanted to remind him that it had been his dad who'd betrayed him by trying to pay her off. His dad had made the decision that they weren't suited. That they needed time to figure out who they were and what they really wanted.

What he'd meant by that, she'd known. Carson needed to go to college and meet someone more suitable. Someone better than the daughter of a small-time rancher who'd died trying to make his way in a sport that had killed him in the end.

She gathered plates and flatware as Derek filled glasses with iced tea. Carson had joined Ruby and Brandon at the table. It was odd seeing him there after so many years. She briefly remembered him at seventeen, all long, loose limbs and charm. Iva had known him forever and had loved his company at family dinners. Ruby had glowed from the inside out when he'd been around. He'd never seemed to mind that worn table, this worn house or the simple meals they'd served. Instead, he'd seemed to fit in, to enjoy his time with them.

Back then Derek had followed him the way Brandon followed him now.

Carson looked up, as if he knew she was watching. He didn't smile. That was the difference between now and then. He seldom smiled now.

"Have they had any more thefts?" Iva asked Carson as Ruby set the table. Derek dropped something in the kitchen. She glanced through the opening and saw him picking up a tub of butter, the contents splattered across the floor.

"You okay in there?" she asked.

"Yeah, just clumsy," he said as he swiped the mess with paper towels.

Ruby turned back to the table. Carson gave her a long look before answering. "I think last night. Someone cut fences over at the Johnson place."

"Where are they taking the cattle and other things they steal?" Iva questioned, half to herself it seemed to Ruby.

"I don't know, but they're hiding it somewhere. Lucy said the sheriff's department is going to take their helicopter up and search the area. They can see more from the air than we can from the ground. We can only go so far with truck, even with ATVs and horses."

"Well, I hope they find them soon. This town can't take much more of this. And I'm about to resign from the league."

"I wish you wouldn't," Carson covered Ruby's grandmother's hand with his. "We need a voice of reason."

"I'm well past being reasonable. I'm ready to retire, Carson. I've been on that league for fifty years. It's time for younger people to take over. People with more energy. Put Ruby in my place."

Ruby sat down across from Carson. "No, thank you. I don't have time or energy for that. Not only that, but I'd get in a fight and then you would have to bail me out."

He smiled at that, and she wanted to tell him it wasn't funny. Instead, she passed him the chicken that had been brought over from the Stillwater cook. He served Iva and Brandon first. Derek had joined them and sat at the opposite end of the table. He scowled a little but then appeared to loosen up and smile.

It felt strange for this to be their family dinner with Carson and Brandon joining them. It wasn't their typical quiet meal; instead, Brandon told stories using sound effects and wild hand gestures. Carson tried to calm him, but the little boy was on a roll. Ruby watched, amused by the two. And she avoided the looks her grandmother gave her from time to time.

And then a glass went over, spilling tea across the table. Brandon let out a shocked, "Uh-oh." Derek jumped up to go after a towel.

"Am I in trouble?" Brandon asked, his bottom lip quivering.

"No, buddy, not in trouble." Carson took the towel from Derek and cleaned up the mess. "But I think we do need to remember to move the glass back from the edge of the table and out of reach."

"I got wild, didn't I?"

"Yeah, just a little. But we're working on that, aren't we?"

Ruby watched, wishing Carson Thorn wasn't so nice to little children and puppies. It would be easier to stay angry if he wasn't so kind. At that moment he stood and wiped the ice and liquid on to his empty plate. He carried it to the kitchen.

Derek passed a piece of pie to Brandon. "You know what will make you feel better? Pie. And guess what else?"

Brandon shrugged. "I don't know."

"We're having a special carnival at church next Sunday afternoon. We're going to have a storyteller who dresses up like people from the Bible. And then we'll have games and food. Want to come?"

Brandon let his gaze fall on Carson, who had just returned from the kitchen.

"I don't know if we can." Carson answered the unasked question. "It depends on what comes up at the ranch. If things are slow, maybe we can slip away for a few hours."

"I'm always available to help if you need someone on a weekend, Carson," Derek offered.

Ruby bit down on her bottom lip, amazed that her brother had the courage to ask. Carson didn't sit back down. Instead, he stood behind Brandon's chair.

"I could use some help from time to time, Derek. This past weekend I could have used someone to go with my trainer when he hauled horses for me."

"I'd be willing to go."

Carson nodded. "Time for us to go, big 'un. We have to check on that new foal and hit the sack early."

Brandon scooted out of his chair. "Oh, I forgot about him. Ruby should come and see him, because he's the prettiest horse ever."

"Ruby is welcome to come see him," Carson said. "And we'll see about church."

As he spoke, Carson gathered up more dishes and headed through the door into the kitchen.

"Carson, leave that for us." Iva called out as he disappeared from sight.

"I don't mind. I really appreciated you letting us stay. The ranch is pretty quiet with just the two of us. We were going to eat at the Little Horn Steakhouse until you offered dinner."

He reappeared, standing in the wide door between the two rooms the way he had years ago. Ruby stood. "I should go out and make sure the barn is locked up."

"Let me help you with that," Carson offered. "Brandon and I are heading that way anyway."

"Can I stay with Derek?" Brandon asked.

Carson looked from the little boy to Ruby's brother. Derek shrugged a slim shoulder. "Sure thing. I'm going to clear the table and load the dishwasher. Brandon can help me out."

"Behave." Carson squatted in front of the little boy. "And be helpful."

Brandon nodded, his eyes big. "And I won't spill anything."

"Spilling isn't the end of the world, kiddo."

And with that Carson and Ruby walked out the back door together. As they walked out she heard Derek telling their grandmother that he'd clean up and she could rest.

Iva didn't argue.

"She's starting to accept this," Ruby said as they walked to the barn.

"It seems that way. But she won't go down without a fight."

"No, she won't." Ruby opened the barn door and Carson held it for her. She switched on a light. The dog, a blue heeler name Chet, raced in ahead of them. "Thank you for taking Derek's offer to help."

"I don't mind. There's always need for an extra hand."

"Of course." Ruby checked the stalls. All empty, the way they should be. She latched the doors from the inside. She locked the tack room door. They didn't have much and it wasn't the best quality, but they couldn't afford to lose anything.

When she turned, Carson was standing close behind her. She looked up, meeting his dark eyes, shadowed in the dim interior of the barn. The air was heavy and warm, and smelled of hay and animals.

His hand brushed her cheek, and she closed her eyes at the familiar touch. Too familiar. Too heartbreaking. She shook her head slightly and tried to move away but he caught her, his hand on hers.

He pulled her close and leaned. And she didn't want him to kiss her. But she did. She wanted him to hold her. She wanted that more than anything. Because in his arms she'd always felt safe. She'd felt as if someone would protect her and she wouldn't always have to be strong on her own, fighting for her family, protecting her brother. Someone else would be there with her.

And then he hadn't been. She reminded herself of that truth as a way to convince her heart that this moment couldn't happen.

It did happen, though. He cupped her cheek and then spread his hand, holding her steady as he leaned, placing his lips against hers. His fingers delved into her hair. His other hand still held hers, keeping her close.

The kiss, slow and easy, transported her back to the girl she'd been, and she wanted to stay in his arms.

But she wasn't that girl. She couldn't be that girl.

The woman she'd become, the one who had been hurt, left to make her own way and now had a family that needed her more than ever, pulled back from him. She shook her head as she broke the kiss and she pulled her hand free from his as she stepped back.

No. She wanted to say it forcefully, with conviction. The word wouldn't move past her lips. Instead, she looked up at him, wondering if that was regret in his eyes.

"Go home, Carson."

He left her alone. The dog, unfaithful beast, followed him. Ruby sat on an overturned bucket and wondered what it would have been like to grow up in a family where she hadn't always had to be the one making the right decisions. What if she'd had the kind of parents who'd done the grown-up thing while she'd lived the life of a normal teen?

That hadn't been her life. And she wouldn't undo what she had. She had Gran. She had Derek. She had a career and a home. She had life experiences that had taught her so much.

She waited until she heard Carson's truck start before she left the barn and headed to the house.

Chapter Six

Carson stood in the center of the arena, the bay quarter horse on a long line that he held in in his gloved hand. He pushed his hat back and wished it would cool off. October should have been cooler. But it seldom was. From the fence Derek Donovan watched, leaning his arms on the top rail. The kid had showed up earlier that day, just to hang out. Carson had allowed him to stay. If he was here, he couldn't get in trouble elsewhere.

He whistled and the horse came to a stop, standing without moving. Carson walked to the animal, coiling the rope as he went. He reached the gelding and the horse turned to look at him just a little, nudging his head against Carson's arm. He pushed the horse away, checked the saddle on his back to make sure it was tight.

"You going to do that yourself?"

Carson looked up, nodding in the direction of Ben Stillwater, who had appeared out of nowhere. He hadn't heard a truck. Ben must have ridden over from his place. He'd been doing that since he'd been old enough to saddle a horse. The few years' difference in their ages hadn't kept the two from being friends.

Even if Ben was a little on the wild side, Carson had always liked him. Maybe it was the difference in their personalities that had made them friends. Carson felt his responsibilities like weights shackled to his feet. Ben did his best to ignore responsibility, even though he managed to keep a tight rein at the Stillwater ranch.

"I usually do," he answered Ben.

Ben stood next to Derek, his hat off, his hair curling in the heat. He glanced at the younger man. "Think he'll get tossed?"

Derek shook his head. "No, he can ride him. Maybe."

"Thanks for the vote of confidence, you two."

Ben laughed. "Always willing to support a friend. So, I just came from town."

"And?" Carson unsnapped the lead rope and led the horse to the fence. He hung the looped long line over a post.

"You won't believe it." Ben gave the gelding a good once over. "That's not a bad looking animal."

"He's going to be a champion cutting horse," Carson assured his neighbor.

"You always think you've got a champion something or other. Remember that old Angus bull you had back in high school? You wanted to show him and your dad wouldn't let you."

"Yeah, I remember. What were you going to tell me about town?"

"Oh, yeah, someone stole the Welcome To Little Horn sign."

"Why in the world would anyone want the town sign?" Carson adjusted the reins and reached for a stirrup. The horse shifted a little, moving away from him.

"He's going to get thrown," Ben said in an aside to Derek.

"Could you focus?" Carson asked. He led the horse in a circle and shot Ben a look.

"Well, it isn't like I know why anyone would want that old sign. It isn't like it's worth anything."

Derek cleared his throat. "Kids. I really think the thieves are kids."

"Why do you think that?" Ben asked, one booted foot on the bottom rail of the arena fence.

"Because they're doing crazy stuff that'll get

them caught. If you want to steal cattle, why would you take stupid chances?"

Ben nodded. "Yeah, I guess. That or someone who wants everyone to think it's a kid."

Carson led the horse to the center of the arena, away from Ben and any temptation he might feel to make good on his theory that Carson would get thrown.

He put a foot in the stirrup and pulled himself up, putting weight on the saddle. The horse stood if he'd been a saddle horse his entire life. Carson swung his leg over and eased his booted foot into the opposite stirrup. The horse shifted under his weight but eased into a walk when Carson gave him a careful nudge.

They made it around the arena. Carson relaxed a little but maintained his control of the reins. With Ben around he wasn't taking any chances. But nothing happened. The gelding didn't take one wrong step. He pulled the horse to a halt at the center of the arena and shot Ben a look, because he'd won.

He settled in and gave the horse a nudge. The big gelding hopped a little. Carson spoke to him in soft, even tones, pushing him past a walk and into a trot. The horse tensed and shook his head. His ears went back. An uneasy feeling swept through Carson. The horse started to shift a little and he could feel his back arching beneath the saddle.

"I think I'd call it a day before you make me the winner," Ben called out. His tone more serious than his words.

Carson shook his head. "If I get off, he'll think this is how we end every ride."

"Carson," Derek said in a low voice. "There's something wrong."

Famous last words. The horse went from tense to bucking, his back end coming up hard and heavy. Carson fought for control, nearly had it and then the animal shifted directions on him.

Carson hit the ground hard. He rolled away from flying hooves and the horse ran to the other end of the arena, still shaking. Ben and Derek were climbing the fence, heading his way.

"I did not do that," Ben called out, hands in the air. "Seriously, Carson, I don't know what happened."

"And I'm supposed to believe you," Carson grumbled at Ben. He shot Derek a look as he moved to his knees, took a deep breath and pushed himself to his feet. "Well?"

Derek shook his head. "He was just standing there. I honestly think it was a bee or something that spooked him."

"I need to get back on him." Carson rolled his shoulders and headed for the horse. "I still think you did this, Stillwater. I don't know how, but you did."

"I really didn't. Here, let the kid get on. You're walking like you're ninety years old."

"I got dumped," he grouched at his friend. "And I can ride my own horse."

"Of course you can. Where's Brandon?" Ben asked as he reached for the reins of the horse.

"My housekeeper Bobbi Ann is watching him. Why?"

"In case you're unconscious. It wouldn't be good to have the kid somewhere and not know where." Ben smirked as he said it.

"You're real funny." Carson took the reins from his ex-friend and managed to get back in the saddle.

"That looked painful." Ben stood next to the horse's head. "I think I'd only give him one opportunity to throw me today. He looks like he's about to blow again. Are you sure there isn't something under that saddle blanket?"

"There's nothing under my saddle blanket. I always check my tack." Carson eased the horse forward a few steps, ran a hand down his neck and he felt the horse start to hunch. "Something's wrong."

He managed to get off before the horse started

to jump and try to get away. The gelding's ears were twitching and his eyes were wild.

"I told you," Ben said. "And you thought I'd try to get you tossed. I only like to win if I win fair."

"Since when?" Carson handed him the reins and he reached for the saddle. He unbuckled the girth strap and hauled the saddle off the horse's back.

Derek grabbed the blanket. He ran his hand over it and stopped about midway back. "Someone is out to get you."

"What?" Ben leaned in close to get a look.

Derek reached between the layers of the folded blanket and pulled out a push pin. He held it up and Carson took it from him.

"Maybe they did that the other day when they took the trophies?" Ben offered.

"Maybe." Carson ran his hand down the horse's still quivering back. "Sorry about that, old man."

The horse turned, rubbed his head against Carson's arm.

"No hard feelings?" Carson shook his head. "If I find out who did that, I'm going to stick pins in their backs."

"You think more than one person?" Derek asked.

"Yeah, I'm starting to think so. Maybe

we're dealing with two different sets of thugs. Thieves and pranksters?"

"Could be," Ben said.

"Let me brush him down for you." Derek took the reins. "I really don't mind."

"Thanks, Derek. Put him in the first stall when you're done, and give him a scoop of grain from the blue bin in the feed room."

"I can do that." Derek walked off with the horse.

Ben opened the gate. "And maybe you should go take advantage of that hot tub on your back deck."

"You act like I haven't been thrown before." Carson limped along next to Ben.

"I know you've been thrown plenty of times."

"I wouldn't say plenty." Carson's pride had to argue.

Ben raised a brow. "Okay, not plenty. A few times. But you are getting older."

He shot his friend a look. "Why did you say you're over here?"

"Can't a neighbor stop by to visit?" Ben slowed his pace. "I don't mind giving you a hard time, but are you sure you're okay?"

"I'm fine."

"Well, I know you wouldn't want to admit in front of Ruby's little brother that…"

Carson stopped walking and pointed to the

horse still tied at his barn. "Why don't you go home?"

"It can't be easy, having her back here."

"It isn't that difficult. We're not kids anymore."

"No, that's for sure." Ben paused, rubbing a thumb along his chin. "She's pretty easy on the eyes. And you've got to be lonely in that big old house."

"I'm not lonely. I have Brandon."

"Right, an eight-year-old."

"He's five," Carson corrected.

A truck rattled up the drive, ending the conversation. And giving Ben Stillwater another reason to laugh. "Well, look who came to call. If it isn't Ruby Donovan?"

"Shut up and go home."

Ben didn't make a move to leave. Instead, he shifted his glance from the rusted-out red farm truck back to Carson. "Carson, some men, like myself, enjoy being single. There are a lot of women in the world and I'm not ready to settle down with just one of them. But you, on the other hand. It's like you had a fortress here with no one to talk to but the walls until that kid came along. That isn't good for a man."

"It serves me just fine."

Ben nodded in the direction of Ruby as she

got out of her truck. "Maybe time to let bygones—"

"Go home."

Ben laughed as he walked away. "Sure thing, friend. But remember, it isn't good for a man to be lonely."

"No, but it does make his life a lot less complicated," Carson shot back as he walked on down the drive to the woman in question. She was a complication. No ifs, ands or buts. But one thing he'd learned when she'd left town was that emotions couldn't be trusted. His had been tied up with her, and that hadn't gotten him too far.

These days he trusted what he knew, not what he felt.

When he reached Ruby, she gave him a careful look head to toe.

"Are you okay?"

He yanked off his hat. "I'm fine."

She blanched at his growl. "Sorry for asking."

Carson closed his eyes briefly, took a deep breath and managed to open his eyes and be a little more human. "I'm sorry. What can I do for you?"

"I'm checking to see if my brother is here."

"He's putting a horse up for me. I can get him and send him home." He started to turn back to the barn but she put a hand on his arm to stop him.

"No, that's okay. I don't want him to think…"

"That you're checking on him?"

She bit down on her bottom lip. "Yeah. I trust him, Carson. But I want to know where he is at all times so that the people who don't trust him can't hurt him with their accusations."

"I understand that. I'm thinking this will all settle down in time and we can all relax again."

"I hope so," she said. And then she glanced at his leg again. "Are you sure you're okay?"

"I'm good. I'm breaking a gelding and…" He didn't want to admit it. Not that he was too proud to say it, but a man did have a code to live by.

"You got tossed!"

"You don't have to sound so happy about it."

She swallowed what looked like the beginning of a smile and her eyes widened, humor lighting the hazel depths. "No, of course I'm not. Maybe we should go inside and get you a glass of tea and some aspirin."

"I'm heading that way now." He kept walking, rolling his shoulders to relieve the kink in his back.

"I should go then."

He was at the steps to the porch and he turned to look at the woman standing in his yard. The wind caught the soft auburn hair, blowing a few tendrils in her face. She looked nervous. She looked out of place. He guessed she would feel all of those things here at his house.

She'd never been inside. It hit him hard. Back when they'd dated his dad wouldn't let her come inside. He'd thought that would keep the two of them apart, if he did everything he could to make Ruby feel unwelcome.

"Come inside?" he offered now. Because he wasn't that kid anymore. It was his home. Looking at her standing in the yard he realized that, if nothing else, she was his friend.

"Okay."

She joined him, walking up the steps and across the wide front porch. He held the door open and motioned her inside. Into his home. And strangely, back into his life in a way she'd never been before.

Carson's home. She'd always wondered what it looked like. She'd always known that if she ever entered through those doors, she would feel out of place. And she did. The entry led to a big living room with windows overlooking the front lawn. The furniture was red leather and oak. The pictures on the walls were expertly placed and expensive.

"How's your grandmother?" he asked as they walked through the living room.

"Not good," she admitted. "The last couple of weeks, it's as if the Parkinson's has gotten a good hold and she's deteriorated. She still tries to do everything she's always done, but I can tell it takes a lot out of her."

"I'm sorry. She's always been strong and I know it's going to be hard. Not just on her, but on everyone who knows her."

She nodded, but she couldn't say more, not with tears stinging her eyes. She was glad his back was to her as they walked through the house.

He led her down a hall to the kitchen with its massive six-burner stainless steel stove, double-door fridge and granite countertops. The cabinets were dark. The floors were stone. The rest of the room was all metal and wood and warmth.

"I think even I could cook in a kitchen like this," she said as he headed for the sink. He leaned to rest both hands on the counter and he straightened his arms to stretch his back. She moved forward, her feet taking her where her mind told her she shouldn't go.

Before she could stop herself her hands rested on his shoulders. She massaged deep into the tissue, and he rolled his head forward, sagging a little but flinching when she hit a tender spot. She started to pull away.

"No, don't stop."

She continued to massage. He straightened, and she rubbed her hands once down his strong, muscled back before stepping away. He turned, sighing and leaning a hip against the counter.

"Thank you."

She shrugged it off, as if it hadn't mattered. As if touching him, being near him after all these years, didn't bother her. He obviously wasn't bothered. Carson was Mr. Composure. She could do that, too; she could pretend it didn't matter.

Even when he stepped close, so close she could smell the outdoors on him, smell the soap he'd used, the aftershave he'd splashed on that morning, the scent of his skin after working horses, even then she told herself she could be composed. But her heart stuttered at his nearness, calling her a liar.

She drew in a breath and looked up, meeting his eyes, dark and questioning. He leaned, and she started to shake her head. But his hand brushed hers, his fingers gently pulling her to him.

The doorbell rang. She let out the breath she'd held. "Saved by the bell," she quipped.

His mouth turned, revealing his dimple. "If you want to see it that way."

"I'll pour the tea," she offered. "If that invitation still stands?"

"It stands. I'll be back."

He came back a few minutes later with her brother in tow. Derek shot her a look. And then he let his gaze settle on Carson in a none-too-friendly way. She didn't need for him to be her watchdog. She'd have to tell him that later. She was fully capable of taking care of herself. She'd been doing it a long time.

Fortunately, a ruckus from the back of the house swept away the awkwardness that lingered among the three.

Carson had pulled three glasses out of the cabinet. He reached for another and a small plastic cup with a lid. "That would be Bobbi Ann and Brandon. She's a great housekeeper, and she doesn't seem to mind double duty as a babysitter in the afternoons."

"If there are days she can't watch him, he's more than welcome to get off the bus at our place," Ruby offered. And then realized she shouldn't have. She shouldn't keep taking these disastrous steps into his life, making offers that only reminded her of how it felt to leave this town and her family with a heart so broken there were still pieces missing.

Pieces he held and he didn't know he held. Or he didn't care. She wanted to ask him what had happened to make him this cold, composed person. What had taken away the laughter, the warmth?

But she wouldn't because he held the pieces and unless he wanted to give them back, she couldn't risk losing more of herself to this man.

Chapter Seven

Carson hadn't been to church much over the years, not since his mom died. On Sunday morning he sat in his truck in the parking lot, Brandon buckled in the backseat of the Ford King Ranch. More than fifteen years had passed since Lila Thorn had left this earth. He missed both of his parents in different ways. His dad had driven him to always succeed. In school. In sports. In college.

His mom had been the soft touch in their lives, always trying to smooth things over when James went too far with discipline and expectations. She'd taken Carson and Jenna to church because it had mattered to her that they have faith. He smiled, remembering how she'd always dressed up when she'd gone out in public. Faith mattered, but appearances mattered, too. She'd been the daughter of a wealthy businessman from Houston. A man Carson barely remembered.

His grandfather had been busy, dedicated, driven.

Sitting in his truck, looking at the white church that people in Little Horn knew as the cornerstone of their community, he thought about that drive and dedication, so much a part of his own life.

Hard work won't let a man down, his dad had always said. Everything else will. When James Thorn had paid off Ruby, he'd used her as an example. "Hard work, son, not emotions."

He thought back on that moment and wondered about his dad's emotions when he'd lost the love of his life. Maybe that was why he'd become consumed with work, with the ranch, with keeping his kids on the path he'd claimed was best. Because emotions hurt.

James Thorn had been too strong to admit to pain.

Carson shook himself free from memories and looked in the backseat at the little boy who had his own pain, a mom who had called only twice—and those conversations had been brief.

Jenna had been a little lost since their mother passed away. Carson had watched her move from one bad relationship to another, losing herself along the way. But she'd always tried to be a good mom. She'd done her best considering she didn't really have someone to lean on. And even though she'd lived at the ranch from time to time, in the past she'd refused to lean on him, to let him help.

As much as he loved his sister, Carson knew that Brandon needed stability. Until he could sit Jenna down and figure out a plan, he had to plan for Brandon's future. He'd called a lawyer this past week to file for guardianship. Because someone had to be in charge. A child couldn't drift with no one being responsible.

"Ready?" Carson asked.

Brandon didn't have a single case of nerves. Instead, he had a big smile and his seat belt was already off. "Yeah. I'm going to learn about Noah's ark. And then there's a carnival."

"Yeah, that sounds like good stuff, doesn't it?"

Brandon nodded as he climbed over the seat. "Let's go."

Carson opened the door and Brandon followed him out. The little boy tucked his hand in Carson's larger one. The two of them walked toward the church together. The bells were ringing. People were streaming in. It wasn't the only church in town, but he guessed it was the biggest. Towns such as Little Horn were all about church and faith.

"Do you think they have cookies?" Brandon asked as they climbed the few steps to the door.

"I'm not sure. They might."

Carson entered the building and it took him back. Man, it took him back. Pain crashed over him. Wave after wave of pain. He couldn't enter this building without remembering being a fifteen-year-old kid, praying for his mother. And the prayers had gone unanswered.

That had been his take on it. Later, after his mother's funeral, when neighbors had stopped to visit and brought food, Iva Donovan had spoken to him with quiet reassurance. She'd told him that sometimes it seemed a prayer was unanswered, but that was never the case. God hears, she'd told him. God hears and He understands our pain, but He sees the bigger picture. She'd told him that for reasons they couldn't understand, God had taken Lila Thorn home. And God would get him through the pain.

Carson had been angry, and he'd bottled that pain up and gotten himself through. He'd used all of that pent-up anger on the football field. He'd used it in basketball and he'd used it on the back of horses.

He felt Brandon pulling on his hand and he looked down at the little boy.

"I have to go to class," Brandon whispered, looking around. "Derek said there's a class."

"Of course." Carson headed for the door that led to the classrooms. "This way."

He didn't make it. Ruby appeared, looking nervous and worried as she reached for Brandon's hand. "I'll take him."

She shot him another look. He let go of Brandon's hand and watched as she hurried away with his nephew.

Emotion can't be trusted. His father's lesson, ingrained from years of hearing the lecture. Carson sank into a pew and pretended he wasn't there for the first time in years. He sang the songs. He listened to the sermon.

He saw himself as a boy praying at the altar, his mother next to him. She'd encouraged his faith. His dad had said it was a crutch.

A thought whispered through his mind, asking him how he'd been doing without faith. He didn't answer because he didn't want to delve that deeply into his life. He existed. The ranch was profiting. He had friends.

Ruby reappeared and sat next to him.

He had friends.

The fall carnival was set up on the big lawn that surrounded the church. Derek had been telling the truth. There were two bounce castles, pie-eating contests, games with prizes, a clown, music and a speaker. Hamburgers were being cooked on big grills. All the sides were set out on tables.

Carson led Brandon in the direction of the food. "Eat first and then play."

"But I had cookies."

Carson had to grin at that argument. "Yeah, well, I think you should have something more than sugar."

"They had nuts," Brandon argued.

"Good argument, but no." Carson knew how to dig in his heels, too. And with a five-year-old around, he was getting better all the time.

"My mom said you'd be strict and I wouldn't be able to get away with arguing."

"Is that so?" he responded, not sure what else to say. How did he reassure a little boy that his mom had promised she'd be back soon? In their last conversation, right before she'd hung up, Jenna had said something about mistakes, but she would be home and things would be better. She promised. They reached the food and he handed Brandon a plate with a burger. "Get chips, some kind of salad and milk to drink."

"But they have cookies." Brandon reached for chocolate chip.

"No." Carson placed watermelon on his nephew's plate.

"Man, that isn't fair." Brandon looked at the fruit. "I think I'm allergic."

"No, you aren't. You had watermelon a few days ago."

"Oh, yeah."

Carson laughed, because having Brandon around made laughing easy. "Go find us a seat."

He watched the little boy hurry away and then he started on his own plate. Byron McKay walked up behind him, his own plate already filled with food.

"Byron," Carson greeted and hoped it would be enough.

"Carson, good to see you here."

"It's good to be here," he said, and it was the truth. But he wouldn't go into that with Byron.

"Is that your nephew over there with Derek Donovan?" Byron nodded in the direction of Brandon and Derek. The two were at a picnic table together. Ruby was nowhere to be seen. Not that he was specifically looking for her.

"You know it is, Byron."

"Do you think that's wise, to let a little boy buddy up to an ex-con who is probably responsible for stealing from your neighbors?"

Carson had to look away from the other man and take a pretty deep breath to keep from saying something that the good Lord wouldn't like to hear on a Sunday. At church.

He turned back to the other rancher and

pinned him with a glare. "Byron, in all of the years I've known you, I've tiptoed around your…" He paused and took another deep breath. "This is church. And you're an elder in this church. And as far as I know, this is the place where we all come for mercy and redemption. It isn't a place where people come for your judgment. Derek Donovan made a mistake, but he's doing his best to stay on the right track. As far as I can tell, you haven't changed a bit over the years."

He turned to walk away and walked right into Ruby Donovan with her big hazel eyes and a tear streaming down her cheek. He shook his head and kept walking. He wasn't a hero. He was just being honest.

Of course she followed him to the picnic table where Brandon and Derek were finishing their lunch. She didn't say anything as he took a seat and she sat opposite him. Derek picked up his empty plate and reached for Brandon's.

"Care if I take him to the bounce house?" Derek asked, smiling at the little boy who was already bouncing.

"No, have at it. And Brandon, in a little while, you and I will shoot some basketballs and see if we can win a prize," Carson offered. Brandon's face split in a big grin.

Carson got a hug that he hadn't been prepared for. Brandon's skinny arms wrapped around him and squeezed tight. And then he was gone, holding Derek's hand as they crossed the lawn.

"Thank you for taking up for my brother," Ruby said a few minutes later.

"I wasn't taking up for him. I was telling the truth."

She placed a hand on his arm. "Yes, the truth. But it matters that you would do that for him."

"I..." He looked down at her hand on his arm and she moved it. "I did what was right, Ruby. He hasn't been caught with any of the stolen property. He's a good hand at my place. Everyone deserves a second chance."

At his words, she looked away but not before he saw the flash of guilt in her hazel eyes. The check, he knew that was what she was thinking about. Someday they would have to discuss it, deal with it.

Not today. He'd already done enough dealing with the past for one day.

Ruby let it go. She didn't want to talk about second chances or the past. Why go there when it was obvious it wouldn't get them anywhere? Instead, she removed herself from Carson's presence, telling him she had to check on Iva.

As she wandered off she did glance back. She pretended she didn't care that he was sitting alone. She pretended it didn't matter that he'd taken up for Derek.

What mattered was that she was a Donovan. And they'd never been good enough. They'd worked hard and scraped to get by, doing their best. But they hadn't been good enough for a Thorn, or for people such as Byron McKay.

She'd heard the whispers in high school, people wondering what Carson saw in Ruby.

She could have told them. She'd made him laugh and forget for a little while that he was hurting. They'd been two broken kids and somehow they'd made a whole.

And she hadn't felt whole since he'd left. Since she left.

They'd completed each other. She'd known it then. She still knew it.

She found her grandmother under the shade of a tree. Iva, surrounded by friends, looked lost. She had a plate of food in front of her and a glass of sweet tea. But something was wrong.

Ruby sat next to her. "How's your lunch, Gran?"

Iva turned to look at her, the movement costing her as her head jerked to the side and her left arm reacted with a sudden twitch. Ruby placed a hand on her grandmother's arm. The two looked into each other's eyes. No words needed.

Ruby picked up a fork and speared a bit of salad. She raised it to Iva's lips. In the past week they'd had a few moments like this. She knew it bothered her grandmother to be dependent this way. If they didn't talk, didn't ask or mention it, they could shuffle through and make do.

Iva ate a few bites of food and then reached for her glass, her hand shaking. Ruby reached into her purse and pulled out a straw. She unwrapped it and placed it in the cup for her grandmother, and Iva leaned to take a sip.

When Iva finished taking a drink she shook her head and leaned toward Ruby. "Getting old stinks."

Ruby smiled. "Yes, Gran, I know it does."

Iva winked. "I'm getting worse, Ruby. We have to face that."

"We'll face it. Together. The way we face everything." Ruby put an arm around Iva and gave her a loose hug.

"Yes, together. Would it be too much for you to take me home?"

"Of course I can take you home. Are you okay?" Ruby studied her grandmother's face. "Should I get Doc Grainger?"

Iva chuckled, the sound raspy and shaky.

"No, honey, I'm just tired. I'm fighting this body every day, trying to win, and it wears me out."

"I'll take you home. Let me see if Derek is ready to go."

She started to get up and when she turned, Carson stood behind her. "I'll get Iva to the truck, and you let Derek know you're leaving. I can give him a ride home if he isn't ready to go."

"You don't have to." Ruby tried to argue but he gave her that serious look of his, forcing her to stop.

"Ruby, I don't mind."

She pulled him away from her grandmother and the other women at the table who would love nothing more than to overhear a conversation they could repeat later.

"Carson, it's too easy."

"Too easy?" He shook his head as he repeated her words.

"Yes, to rely on you. To have you back in my life. It's too easy. You make it too easy. My…" She stopped. She had almost said *heart*. She couldn't say that word.

"I'm a neighbor, Ruby. And I'm offering to help get your grandmother to your car."

"I know." She had to look away from probing dark eyes or she'd get lost in them.

"I'm going to take your grandmother to your car. If you want to find an argument to stop me, go ahead, but remember that this isn't about us. It's about Iva. We can agree on that, can't we?"

"Yes, we can."

And she watched him walk back to her grandmother. He whispered something, and Iva smiled and nodded. As she stood there, helpless against her heart, Carson Thorn scooped her grandmother into his arms and headed across the lawn with her.

All of her arguments with herself about him, about being a Donovan and not good enough, were lost when Carson acted like a man willing to come to the rescue.

Chapter Eight

Ruby stood in the tack room looking at the saddles. One saddle was adult sized, the leather soft
and beautiful, the stitching like nothing she'd
ever experienced. The other three saddles were
for ponies. They were sitting on stands with bridles hung over the saddle horns. She touched
the seat of the larger saddle and then pulled her
hand away, because these saddles weren't hers.

She hadn't noticed them earlier in the day
when she'd been out here feeding, before she'd
gone to fix the fence at the back of the property. She guessed she hadn't been in the tack
room for a couple of days. There hadn't been
a reason to come in here, so she didn't really
know when the saddles had shown up.

Sunday. She'd been out here Sunday. It was
Tuesday.

Not Derek. She wouldn't let herself believe

he'd done this, that he'd either stolen the saddles or bought them with money from stolen merchandise.

The previous night he'd come home with new boots. She'd asked him where he'd got boots like that, obviously expensive, more than they could ever afford. He'd smiled and said the boots were a gift.

An expensive gift. Maybe the saddles were a gift, too.

She didn't know what she'd do if Derek was involved. And she didn't want to lose faith in him, in the changes she'd seen in him.

The door to the tack room opened. She jumped back from the saddles and spun to face Carson. He looked from her to the saddles. And he didn't say anything.

For a brief second she let herself believe the saddles were from him. After all, he knew she needed tack for the riding school.

"New saddles?" he asked, blowing her theory.

"Yes, they are. They…" They'd just appeared overnight.

He stepped into the room, followed by Brandon. She glanced at her watch, surprised that it was after four in the afternoon. She'd forgotten they had another lesson scheduled.

"Brandon, look at your new boots." She exclaimed over the new boots he was making every effort to show off.

"Thanks. And I sure like that saddle."

"I bet you do. You pick one and we'll saddle up the horse for you to ride."

Carson stood off to one side, watching her, then looking at the saddles.

"Stop, Carson. Don't look at me like that."

He shrugged one shoulder. "I'm not looking at you. But those aren't cheap saddles, Ruby."

"You think I don't know that?"

"Sis, you in here?" Derek appeared at the door. He saw the saddles and whistled. "Wow, Carson, is that a makeup gift?"

"'Makeup gift'?" Carson didn't look amused.

Ruby cringed, knowing that Derek would say too much, and knowing that stopping her brother would be like trying to jump in front of a train and stop it with her bare hands. Derek stepped into the crowded tack room, his attention focused on the saddles.

"Derek…" she started.

He whistled as he ran his hand over the leather. "Yeah, you know, for all of the rotten things your sister said about her."

"My sister?" Carson's words came out low, controlled.

She knew that controlled tone. She looked up, met his gaze with a strong look of her own.

"Time for riding lessons. Come on, Brandon, pick a saddle."

Oblivious, the little boy reached for the darkest saddle, claiming it as his own. She lifted it from the stand and carried it out of the room, away from the men, away from the tension.

"I think you're ready for an easy lope," she informed the little boy as she settled the saddle on a rail and grabbed a lead rope off the hook on the wall.

"Seriously?" Brandon started to jump and she stopped him.

"Only if you're calm."

He took a deep breath and nodded. "Calm," he repeated.

She smiled at the instant and exaggerated calm and led him outside to catch his pony. When they returned with the little bay, Derek was waiting to help saddle. He took the lead rope from her.

"Sorry, sis, I'm afraid Carson didn't like what I said. I think he's waiting to talk to you."

"I'm not in the mood to talk." She glanced around and saw that they were alone. "Where did the saddles come from, Derek?"

"Like I know? I thought Carson gave them to you to help you out. Guess not."

"No, he didn't."

"Sis, I hope you don't think I—" He paused

in the process of slipping the bridle on the pony. "You thought I did it?"

"No, I didn't. I don't know."

"I need you to believe in me," he said, finishing with the bridle. "Go talk to Carson."

She nodded and started to walk away. Brandon was standing there, watching with big eyes and a knowing look. Ruby turned back to her brother. "Derek, I'm sorry."

"I know you are."

She walked out of the barn. Carson stood near the corral, his arms crossed over the top rail. She stopped next to him.

"What was that about?" he asked.

Would it work to pretend she didn't know what he meant by that question? A quick glance at his stern features, the straight line of his mouth and the dark eyes focused on the horizon, and she knew she wouldn't be able to pretend this away.

"History. Ancient history."

"So, you won't tell me what Jenna did, or what she said?"

She could, but what would it matter? "Carson, I don't want to go back to those days, to the girl I was. I don't want to relive those times."

"No, I guess you don't. Neither do I," he admitted. "But those saddles are a problem."

"I know they are. And I know how it looks."

He did glance down then, his gaze connecting with hers, making her feel all kinds of confused. She wanted to defend her brother. She wanted to tell him how much Carson had hurt her. She wanted… She shook her head. Not him. She did not want him.

"Do you know how it looks?" he asked. "Do you realize what people will think?"

"Yes, I do. They'll think my brother either took those saddles or that he stole cattle and bought the saddles with ill-gotten gains. But he didn't. And I have so many other things to worry about that I don't want to spend time worrying about what you or the people in this town think about us. I'm way past being the teenage girl who isn't good enough."

He shook his head at the speech. "Tell me how you really feel."

"I feel like I've had enough. I feel like I have more important things to worry about than false accusations." She headed for the gate. "I'm going to give your nephew a riding lesson."

"How's Iva?" His softly spoken question stopped her.

She turned, one hand on the gate. She shaded her eyes with her other hand, glad for the bright light in her eyes that explained the sudden dampness in her eyes and kept her from seeing sympathy in his expression. Hearing it in his voice was hard enough.

"She's okay. Not good but okay. She told me she's going to put herself in the nursing home if I don't do it for her."

"And you said?"

She shook her head. Cars were pulling up. Her other students. "I told her no way will I do that."

"She should know better than to argue with you."

"She should. It's like arguing with herself." She watched the other kids heading their way. Derek and Brandon were already in the arena. "Have you heard from his mom?"

"She called last week and talked to him for a few minutes."

"Where is she?" She paused. "I'm sorry, it's none of my business. But he's a great kid and this has to hurt."

"She's in Austin. She said she's getting her life together. She wants to be a better mom and she knew she was failing."

"If there's anything I can do…" She made the offer, knowing she was putting herself, her own heart, on the line.

"I appreciate that. I told her I'm going to file for guardianship and Brandon can stay with me. She can come home and use the trailer we have empty. When she can prove she's dependable she can have her son back."

"She's willing to do that?"

He watched his nephew getting on the pony. "Yes. She doesn't have a choice. I've watched as she has dragged Brandon from one relationship to another. He needs for her to be present in his life."

"What about his dad?"

"Left with another woman and never looked back. Jenna was married once before him, a guy she met right out of high school."

"She's lost, Carson. I know that isn't an excuse, but she's obviously hurting. Don't be too hard on her." Words she never thought she would utter. Not about Jenna. But time did have a way of making things easier. And as an adult she could see that she and Jenna had a lot in common. The loss of parents. The hole that loss left.

"That's pretty forgiving of you." His voice was low, intent, and it brushed down her spine, making her shiver.

She stepped through the gate, needing distance between them. She had students. She glanced in the direction of the children.

"She let me know where I belong. Or didn't

belong. She let me know what was best for you. Don't worry. She didn't say it to my face."

"She doesn't know what is best for her own son, Ruby."

"I know." She stood in the arena, knowing she had to escape. "I can't talk about this right now."

"Later." He looked at his watch. "I have to run to town. I'll be back when his lesson is over."

She nodded and watched him go. And she breathed, taking the deep breath her lungs needed. Let him go, she told herself. Let him walk away and let him stay in the past. Because he could only hurt her if she cared too much.

And she did.

She cared about him. She cared that he might not trust her brother. She cared that he was alone. Still not whole. Neither of them seemed to be whole.

Carson drove the few miles to town, his mind anywhere but on the road and the work he needed to catch up on for the league. The last thing he really wanted to do was go into that building and hear more complaints. It was a sad day when dealing with that mess appealed to him more than staying at the Donovan place, watching Ruby give riding lessons to a half-dozen kids.

Watching Ruby, though, that would have been torture. Standing at that fence, watching her smile at children, laugh that carefree way she did, maybe talk to a few of the moms who stayed to observe their kids on horseback. If things had been different...

He thought about that. They had planned on getting married when he graduated from college. They used to sit on the back of his truck and talk about their imaginary kids and what they'd name their little boy and how their little girl would look just like her. A boy named Stetson. He smiled now, thinking about that little boy maybe having her hair instead of his. Or his hair and her eyes.

The dreams of kids, just kids who'd had no idea how life would stack up against them. His dad had shown him a copy of the check and told him the money was the only way she would get an education. Carson would go to college and find someone more suitable. As if they lived in a world that cared.

But his dad had cared. He'd been born and raised to care. They were Thorns, after all. They were Texas society. They were politicians and community leaders; there were expectations.

A car honked as he drove through town.

He slowed, nodding to acknowledge that he'd nearly run a stop sign. He waved an apology. The driver offered him an angry glare in return.

Carson sighed and pulled on through the intersection. He paid more attention as he finished the three-block drive to the league headquarters. As he pulled in he noticed several cars and trucks. Yeah, people were here. He couldn't avoid it.

He walked inside, smiled at Ingrid and wished she didn't have that hungry look in her eyes. With a vague greeting he kept walking in the direction of his office. Maybe he should sit Ingrid down and explain that he wasn't interested, and it had nothing to do with her. She was a pretty woman with a lot to offer.

Romance was the last thing he wanted. He didn't want to get sidetracked. He didn't want to make another mistake.

Before he could pour himself a cup of coffee, Ingrid appeared in his office, a plate in hand. "I have fresh-baked chocolate chip cookies."

He dripped coffee on his hand and set the pot down to wipe up the spill. When he turned she was biting on her bottom lip and looking apologetic.

"I didn't mean to scare you."

"You didn't." He tossed the paper towel in

the trash. "That pot always leaks when you pour it."

"If you hold the lid back, it won't. Something about the lid…" she rambled on nervously.

"Ingrid, I'm not interested."

She went pale, and he wanted to swear.

"I mean in the cookies." He pointed to the plate in her hand.

She lit up and that was almost as bad as the rejection. "Oh, okay. Well, if you change your mind…"

He wouldn't. "Thank you."

She left his office. He moved to his desk with a cup of coffee.

"That was about as suave as Byron trying to convince the preacher that he doesn't make change in the offering plate."

Carson looked up. Ben Stillwater stood in the doorway, a big grin on his face.

"Sure, come on in," Carson grumbled. "You know, I can't seem to get a break today. What do you want?"

"Decent conversation and to leave here with my head intact. What's gotten under your skin?" Ben took a seat across the desk from Carson. "Or should I say who?"

"Don't start."

"I won't. I'm not here to give you a hard

time. I saw your truck and thought I'd stop and see if you've heard the news."

At that Carson looked up from the papers on his desk. "Please tell me someone caught the thieves?"

Ben leaned back in the chair. "No, sorry. But now, to top it off, we seem to have a Robin Hood on our hands."

"The saddles?" He already knew about that.

"What saddles?" Ben leaned forward, pulling off his hat and swiping a hand through his too-long hair.

"Ruby found a tack room full of saddles."

"Do you think Derek did it?" Ben asked the obvious question.

"He seemed pretty surprised to see them and thought that I'd done it to make up for something Jenna did."

"Oh, yeah. I'd forgotten about that."

"What?" Carson started to lift his coffee cup, but he set it back down on his desk. The hot liquid sloshed over the sides. He reached for the paper towels that seemed to be a necessity these days.

"I'm not getting into this. But the saddles are interesting because Ruby isn't the only one receiving gifts."

"Get to the point," Carson demanded. He'd always thought of himself as a patient man.

He'd always thought ranching was in his blood and that he'd never leave this town. But these days he was having second thoughts about just about everything. He could almost see himself taking the job he'd recently been offered with the state in the Department of Agriculture. The offer was for a job that would help to develop more agriculture export from the state.

People said politics were tough. But living in a small community wasn't a picnic.

Ben got up and poured himself a cup of coffee.

"Ben," Carson said it as a warning.

Ben grinned as he sat back down. "You need to get yourself a wife. Maybe you'd be less testy."

"Get out." Carson pointed at the door.

His friend just laughed. "I'm getting there. Daniel Bunker woke up to a surprise this morning at the Circle C. There was a note on the corral. *A gift to make things easier.* Some people think the gift was from your ranch because there were ten mighty fine-looking Angus in his corral. But they aren't tagged and don't have your brand."

"I haven't lost…" He groaned, thinking about his cut fence and the cattle he'd just bought. Cattle that wouldn't have his brand.

If they were his cattle, he wasn't taking them back from Daniel.

"Daniel was going to have to file a medical bankruptcy," Ben continued with the story. "He's about done in, paying for cancer treatments for his son. They're getting help now, but the travel and the hotels, the food… It's been a hard year for them."

"We need to do a fund-raiser," Carson interjected. "A plate dinner."

"That would help, too."

"I'll get Ingrid on that."

Ben laughed. "That should keep her busy for a week or so."

"You could ask her out," Carson said in all seriousness.

"No, thanks," Ben said. "I don't always like to date local. Too many people get in a man's business."

"Right." Carson rubbed his thumb across his chin. "Cattle. Saddles. Someone seems to want to do some good deeds. So is it our thieves or is it someone else?"

Lynette Fields appeared in the door of the office before Ben could answer. The former CPA with her no-nonsense short gray hair and always-serious expression didn't smile as she eyed the two of them.

"Pastor Mathers was in here earlier. People

are asking him if it is the church's Here to Help organization that is leaving the anonymous gifts."

Ben laughed at that. "Yeah, because the church is now into regifting stolen merchandise—cattle, hay and what else?"

He looked to Carson for a response, but Carson didn't want to be involved.

"No one says the gifts are stolen, Ben." Lynette, who was the league's treasurer, stepped farther into the room, not at all shy about chastising Ben. Carson kept a straight face.

"No," Ben agreed. "I'd say I know where the cattle came from."

"Let it go," Carson warned. "How are our citizen detectives doing?"

Lynette took the other chair in the room and sat down, her back straight, her serious gaze settling on him. "They've heard you called them a posse. They aren't amused."

"Sorry, but I don't know what else to call them. And the last thing we need is for someone to get shot because we have a bunch of people out trying to hunt down the thieves."

"Well, Tom Horton said they haven't had any luck. He said if they are in one place, the thieves are on the opposite side of the county. As if they know." Lynette relaxed a little, leaning back in the chair.

"That's interesting. We need to let Lucy know so she can pass that on to the state and her deputies." Carson steepled his fingers and let his gaze slide over the paperwork on his desk for a new sign. "I think the sign is a city government issue, not a league issue."

"The league put the sign up to begin with," Lynette informed him.

"I get that but I also know that the league can't step on the toes of the mayor and town council. Maybe we should talk to them and see if they have plans to replace it. Or maybe to wait and see if we get it back."

"I'll have Ingrid call," Lynette agreed. "Some folks in town are wondering if Amelia Klondike might be the one helping people out."

"She could be," Carson agreed. Other than the stolen cattle part. But he wouldn't mention it again. People were looking for explanations and they were going to think what they wanted to think. Amelia did have money. And she seemed to be uncomfortable with keeping it all for herself.

She might buy cattle to help a neighbor. Or she could have just written him a check. People didn't always want explanations that made sense.

Lynette stood. "I have to go see what Fred

wants for dinner tonight. You boys stay out of trouble."

He nodded and watched her go.

"Are we still teenagers?" Ben asked after she'd left the building.

"In her eyes we will always be kids. And some of us still do act…"

Ben shook his head. "Don't you start. I'm not the one circling the Donovan place."

"I'm not circling anything. Ruby is giving Brandon riding lessons." Not that he needed to explain.

Ben, like others, didn't want reasonable explanations.

"Of course that's why you're over there." But then his smile faded. "What do you think about Derek?"

Carson shrugged. "I think the kid is clean and he's doing his best. He's been over at my place helping out."

"And he'd have access to your—"

Carson held up a hand to stop the accusation before it could be fully verbalized. "Don't. He has enough odds stacked against him."

"Yeah, that's true. So you're taking him under your wing?"

"I'm doing what I can for him."

Ben stood to leave. Or at least Carson hoped

that's what he meant to do. "Ruby is a catch, Carson. She always has been."

With that, he left, and Carson didn't have a chance to tell him to mind his own business.

Carson leaned back in his chair and rubbed both hands over his face. Man, he was tired. His life was eating him up, wearing him out. Too many irons in the fire, Iva had once told him. He hadn't agreed back then, but he did now.

What he needed to do was go home and take a long ride. Not the kind of ride that included rounding up cattle, fixing fences and checking a herd.

He was afraid if he took that ride it would lead him down a nearly forgotten trail to the Donovan ranch and a section of fence he'd cut long ago to make a gate between their properties.

He glanced at his watch, reminding himself that he had to pick up Brandon. And that meant facing Ruby all over again.

Chapter Nine

The post office seemed to be the place to be on a Thursday midway through October. Ruby had a few bills to mail so she stood in the long line of customers. The lady at the front of the line, Miss Winters, a retired school teacher, was having a heart-to-heart with the postmistress, obviously not realizing a half-dozen people were behind her.

Ruby smiled at Henry Jepps, a neighbor to the east of the Donovan ranch. He inclined his head and touched a finger to the brim of his hat.

"How's your granny doing, Ruby?" Henry asked as they stood there.

"She's getting by, sir."

"I reckon she is. Iva has always gotten by, hasn't she? She's one strong lady. I remembered when, well, we don't need to go back that far, do we?"

Ruby smiled at that. "She's been through a lot."

"She sure has."

Miss Winters turned to leave the counter. She spotted Mr. Jepps. "Henry, did you hear that the Matherses' place got hit? That's getting a little too close to home."

Henry looked at Ruby, an apologetic turn of his lips as he shook his head. "No, Ella Lee, I hadn't heard that."

"Well, it happened last night. And did you hear that Dora Peterson woke up this morning to ten round bales stacked up next to her barn? She said she won't get through the winter without that hay. But she's afraid to keep it for fear it's stolen property. That's a felony, keeping stolen property."

The saddles. Ruby nearly groaned because she knew that Miss Winters must have heard about the saddles.

"There are ways to check and see if the property has been stolen, Miss Winters." Ruby said it with a lighter tone than she'd believed possible. "Someone left saddles at my place, and they haven't been reported stolen."

"Well, that's fortunate for you that something so needed has appeared at your place, Ruby."

Mr. Jepps gave her an encouraging look before facing Miss Winters. "I'd say it was a blessing. Not only for Ruby, but for Dora. I can't understand who would steal from their neighbors, but I have a healthy dose of respect for the person helping their neighbors."

"There's no such thing as a Robin Hood, Henry Jepps," Miss Winters's voice rose along with the color in her cheeks. "Stealing is wrong and helping neighbors doesn't make it right."

"I agree with that, but I don't think anyone knows for sure that our thieves are Robin Hoods. The two circumstances haven't been connected. They're just happening at the same time."

Miss Winters heaved a breath. "Well, I guess you do have a point. Give Mrs. Jepps my best. And Ruby, tell Iva I'm praying for her."

Miss Winters left. Henry Jepps laughed and put a hand on Ruby's back to move her forward in the line. "I'd dare say your Granny Iva is praying for our Miss Winters, too. The lady hasn't been happy since she was twenty and her soldier boyfriend decided not to come back and marry her."

At that, Ruby turned and watched out the window as Miss Winters got in her car. *She* was Miss Winters. The thought unsettled her.

What if in forty or fifty years she was the angry, bitter woman terrorizing her neighbors?

For a few minutes she'd been relieved to know that others were receiving gifts. It meant that maybe no one would point fingers at Derek. Now she had other worries. She didn't want to be Ella Lee Winters—bitter and alone. And she didn't want her neighbors to believe she'd received stolen property.

She stepped forward to take care of the postage for her mail and to retrieve a package that was too big for her mailbox. The postmistress handed over the package and then rested a hand on hers, stopping her from turning away.

"Ruby, I wanted you to know that we're praying for you all. I know this has been difficult for you, coming home to Iva's failing health." She patted Ruby's hand. "And don't you let the gossips get to you."

"Thanks, Linda. I appreciate that."

"Well, it isn't much, but you let us know if you need anything at all. Vince isn't so laid up that he can't help you out if you need something done out there. I know Derek is able-bodied, but sometimes things pile up on a person."

"Yes," Ruby agreed, sometimes things did pile up.

Right now was one of those times. And it wasn't the work. It was Iva. It was the thefts.

The gossip. And feeling so alone that her heart ached. She couldn't share her concerns with Iva. She definitely couldn't tell Derek. There were days she didn't know if they could keep the ranch going. There were days, or maybe just moments, when she let the suspicions over her brother get to her.

She said goodbye to the postmistress and Mr. Jepps, and left the post office. The sun had gone behind clouds and rain had started to fall, just a light mist that made the air smell of moisture and warm asphalt. With her head down, she came to a sudden stop when strong hands grabbed her arms.

"Are you going to walk off that curb without looking?"

She spun to face Carson and then she glanced back. She had been about to step down off the curb and a car was pulling into what had been an empty space next to her car. She closed her eyes and shook her head.

"I didn't…"

She was not going to cry. She wasn't going to let him know that it was too much. All of it. Iva. Derek. Him. He was too much.

Maybe they should put the ranch on the market and move to Oklahoma. She could get her old job back. She could find a nice house where

Iva wouldn't feel the need to mend, fix and garden. Derek could have a fresh start.

"Ruby, are you okay?"

"Of course I am." She raised her chin a notch and managed to move her mouth into something she hoped reflected that she was good. Everything was fine. She wasn't going to lose it right there on the sidewalk in front of the Little Horn Post Office. Wouldn't the gossips love that?

"That's not a smile. It's a grimace," he informed her.

"Well, I was going for a smile."

He laughed a little. "Good try but you failed. Let's have coffee at Maggie's."

"No, thank you."

He pushed his hat back as he looked down at her. "A piece of pie?"

She shook her head and looked down at the sidewalk. She couldn't look up at him. She didn't want to see this man who had once been the boy she loved. She didn't want him to look too closely for fear of what he'd see in her eyes. And she couldn't face his sympathy right now, not when she was barely holding on to what remained of her composure.

"Something happen in the post office?" Carson asked, moving a little closer.

"No." *Yes.* "I'm just too exhausted to deal with

this town. And if I go to Maggie's, that's what I'll have to deal with."

"So you're going to hide away on the ranch?"

"Yes."

His hand came to rest on her back and somehow they were heading for his truck. The big, dark blue vehicle glistened in the misty rain. The engine was still running.

"I'm not going to Maggie's with you." She tried to dig in her heels. She quickly pulled the keys from her pocket. "I have Iva's Home Shopping Network purchase. She's been waiting for this. Some type of herbal cure-all."

"Maybe it'll help."

"Stop." She pulled away from the comfort of his hand on her back. Not because she didn't want it, but because she was afraid she might need him too much.

"We'll go to the steakhouse and not Maggie's. This time of day there's no one in there."

His offer vibrated over her. For some foolish reason she nodded, and the next thing she knew she was in his truck. The air conditioner was on and it blew against her rain-dampened skin. She shivered, and he reached to turn it down.

"We need some real rain," he observed as he glanced in the mirror to back out of the parking space.

"I know. Believe me, I know. I'd like a good weeklong soaker so I don't have to buy so much hay. If we could get some rain, I know the grass would grow and we'd be in good shape for a little while."

"I have hay," he said. And then he shifted and drove down the street in the direction of the steakhouse. "I can spare a few bales."

"We'll be fine." She meant it. She wasn't merely being stubborn.

"Of course you'll be fine." He pulled into the parking lot of the one restaurant in town other than Maggie's.

They got out of the truck and headed for the entrance of the restaurant. The rain had stopped and the sun had peeked back out. The air was warm and heavy with humidity. Ruby swiped a hand across her brow.

"This is miserable."

"Yeah, it is. Hopefully we won't get a storm out of this. We're supposed to have a cool front coming in sometime tonight."

"I hope by cool you mean real cool and not just the lower sixties."

"Real cool," he answered as he opened the door for her.

She stepped into the dimly lit restaurant aware that Carson stood behind her. His presence was so real, so comforting. The scent of him was familiar, even after all of these years. His touch on her back made her feel safe.

Time went by but the memories hadn't faded. For a couple of short years she'd been Carson Thorn's. He'd been hers. They'd been a whole.

She shook free from thoughts that were dangerous to her heart.

The hostess led them to a table in the corner of the restaurant. She handed them menus, offered them coffee and walked away. Carson looked at the woman seated opposite him. She kept her gaze on the menu but he saw the shadows under her eyes, the weariness in her shoulders.

And he cared. He told himself it was because at one time she'd been important to him. More than important. She'd been everything. It only made sense that he'd still care.

"I'm not here to eat," she said, putting the menu aside. "That isn't why we came here, is it?"

"Yes, we're here to eat."

He put the menu back in her hands and saw the dip of her head. She'd never been fragile. Tiny, compared to him, but not fragile. To him, she'd always been one of the strongest people he knew. She still came off that way. But today he'd seen a chink in her armor.

"Thank you," she said quietly, her head still dipped as she studied the menu.

In the dim light he watched as she swiped at her cheek, removing the single tear that had slid down. He swallowed the crush of emotion that walloped him with that single tear. That's what it took to knock a man to the ground, a tear. One single, solitary tear sliding down a pale face.

He felt destroyed in a whole new way. He'd been crushed when she'd left without saying goodbye. He'd spent years telling himself he didn't care. He'd buried himself in the ranch.

And now, undone by a tear.

"What happened in the post office?" he asked in a quiet voice that seemed too loud in the nearly empty restaurant.

The waitress reappeared. She started to speak, but he waved her away. She scurried away after leaving ice water for each of them. Ruby lifted hers and took a sip.

"Nothing happened," she finally answered.

He arched an eyebrow at the answer and she half-smiled.

"Okay," she admitted. "Miss Winters was in there, and she had to share her opinions on everything."

"She does have strong opinions."

She shrugged slim shoulders. "It was just

one of those last-straw moments. I'm just tired, Carson. I'm worried about my grandmother and about Derek. I actually contacted a Realtor the other day."

"Iva couldn't handle selling that place, Ruby. She's always said that she lost her husband, her son, she nearly lost her grandkids. She couldn't lose that ranch. It's the foundation. It's the place you come back to when everything else lets you down."

She nodded, agreeing. "She's always told us that. But what can I do? I can't support us on what I'm making giving riding lessons. I can't get a job in town and leave Iva alone. Derek has a job, but it's part-time."

"And you're trying to carry the load on your own. You've always done that, you know."

"I know. But there's never been anyone else."

He started to tell her there was someone else. He could have been the person helping her if she hadn't left. Now? As he looked at her, auburn hair framing her face, her eyes dewy, he still wanted to be the person who picked up the pieces for her.

"There's me." He said it reflectively. "I haven't gone anywhere."

"No, you haven't. Here we are, full circle. My family is still trying to get their feet on steady ground. And you…"

He waited.

"You're still strong. You still know who you are. And the last thing you need right now is my family depending on you."

"I've got broad shoulders."

"Yes, you do. And you're taking care of Brandon. He's the important one right now. He needs you."

"I can do more than one thing at a time."

The corner of her mouth lifted, revealing the slightest dimple in her cheek. "I know. And I also know the gossips will eat you alive if you attach your name to ours. This town is determined to hang my brother. They're determined to see me as the gold digger who only wanted money from your father to walk away."

He didn't know what to say to that.

She reached across the table and touched the tips of her fingers to his. He looked at their two hands, his large and suntanned. Hers was dainty for all the work she did, and fair. That little hand couldn't fool him. He knew she was strong.

And she'd just revealed the elephant in the room with them. The check. The last thing he wanted to talk about.

"They'll talk," he admitted. "But I'm offering to help and I don't really care what they say."

"I know, and I appreciate it." She drew in a

breath and sighed. "It isn't the work, Carson. It's worry. I'm worried about Iva and Derek, and of course I'm worried about the ranch. But the ranch is just a thing. It's our home, but we can have a home anywhere. But if I lose Iva or Derek… I'm just not sure what I'd do without them."

"I know." He moved his hand. This required more contact. It required him sliding his fingers through hers, not caring what the gossips said.

She lifted her free hand and covered her eyes. "I'm so sorry."

He didn't know what the apology was for and he didn't question it. She sniffled and pulled free. As he tried to gather his wits, she headed for the front door. He tossed a bill on the table and went after her.

She didn't go far. Not far at all. When he walked outside, she was sitting on the tailgate of his truck. A few tears trickled down her cheeks, and he didn't have a thing to offer. He dug around in the cab of his truck and found a small package of tissues.

When he sat down next to her, he held them out and she took them, wiped her eyes and then blew her nose. She didn't look at him.

"You probably wanted lunch," she said.

"No, not really. What I really want to do is go for a ride."

That got her attention. She looked up. "What?"

"When was the last time you went riding for fun?"

"It's been a long time," she said as she tucked herself against him. He wrapped an arm around her and pulled her closer.

"Yeah, me, too."

"Why?"

He looked down at her. "Busy with the ranch, with life. I ride every day. But days off, those are few and far between."

They sat there a few more minutes before he forged ahead with the invitation. "Go for a ride with me, Ruby. Let's make a picnic lunch and ride to the spring."

"That's a long ride."

He smiled at that. "Yeah, it is. We could leave early, when Brandon gets on the bus for kindergarten and be back by the time he gets home."

"I'm not sure if it's a good idea."

"What isn't a good idea, Ruby? The ride? Or us?"

She hopped down from the tailgate and moved to stand in front of him. "Us."

He wanted to ask why, but he decided maybe

he didn't want the answer. Maybe he'd been right about not trusting emotions. Once again he'd started thinking that together they were a lot better than they were apart.

Chapter Ten

The fence had been cut. Ruby leaned down from her saddle and touched the fence where once upon a time she and Carson had made a hidden gate between their two properties. She'd fixed it a long time ago. But someone had definitely made cuts in the barbed wire. Several strands were hanging loose. Two of the five strands of fence had been reattached, though. As if the thieves almost had gotten caught or maybe had changed their minds.

She swung down off her horse and reached into the saddlebag where she had tools. She'd been working on fences since breakfast, going back to the house for lunch with Iva before heading out to check this last section. She told herself she wasn't keeping busy to keep her mind off Carson and their run-in the previous day. Not a run-in…a moment?

As she stood there, her gaze drifted across the rolling fields in the direction of the Thorn ranch. She hadn't crossed that property line in a dozen years. She remembered the last time well. She and Carson had taken a late-evening ride before he left to go back to school. She'd been in her sophomore year. He'd graduated from high school and still had been trying to make a plan for college.

On impulse she used wire cutters and snipped the two strands of barbed wire. They recoiled, snapping back and leaving an opening. Her horse danced a little away from the snaking wire. She led him through the opening and then she pulled wire out of her bag and quickly fixed the fence. It wasn't perfect, but it would keep their small herd in.

She put her left foot in the stirrup and swung her right leg over the saddle, settling into the seat and heading her horse toward the Thorn home and stables. She didn't give herself time to reconsider; instead, she kept her horse at a steady lope, eating up the rough terrain.

As she neared the stable she saw someone in the arena. A man on the back of a beautiful chestnut. She slowed her horse to a walk. Even from a distance she knew it was Carson. No one rode the way he did, all strength and confidence. He trained cutting horses and he had several champion show horses.

She watched the man on the back of the golden-red chestnut. His face was shaded by the white cowboy hat, but she saw the firm, determined line of his jaw. She could see his mouth in a straight, unwavering line. He wasn't ruggedly handsome. He was all straight lines and perfection. The kind of handsome that took a girl's breath.

He used his knees more than the reins to guide the big animal. The horse was attentive to his gestures and reacted, turning right and then spinning back to the left. Carson looked up, saw her and smiled.

After a few minutes he headed her way. He brought the horse up to the fence and eased him to a stop.

"I didn't expect you today," he said.

She eased her horse forward. "I was checking fence. I…" She stopped.

He waited.

"The old gate," she admitted. "I was actually fixing it because someone cut it."

"They cut the fence between your place and ours?"

"Yeah, I don't know why they'd do that."

He swung his leg over the back of the horse and dropped to the ground. "They hit the Hansens'. Maybe they were confused. Your place, ours, theirs. We do have a triangle. If someone didn't know better, they might get the fences confused."

"So you think the thieves have a conscience? The Hansens have more, so they stole from them and not me?"

"I don't know what else to think," he said as he leaned on the fence, watching her.

"I guess in some strange way it does make sense. And they hit you, too. But no one is talking about those ten head of Angus."

He shrugged one powerful shoulder. "I don't have any cattle missing."

"Okay," she said, but they both knew he did. They both knew that his cattle had been left at the Bunkers', a family desperately in need with hospital bills piling up.

"You ought to take your horse over and give him a drink," he added and pointed to the trough at the front of the stable. "I'm going to cool this guy down and put him out to pasture. Your brother is out helping my guys tag calves."

She nodded and dismounted to lead her horse to the trough. "And where's Brandon?"

"I had to borrow a backhoe from Ben. When I went to take it back, Brandon met Eva and somehow he convinced her to let him stay there. She didn't seem to mind."

"She's a sweetheart," Ruby said as she stood next to her horse, watching Carson walk through the door into the stable. It seemed the lamest thing to say.

Her gelding stuck his nose in the water, swished back and forth a few times and then took a long drink. When the horse finished, as was his habit, he dipped his nose in the water again, swishing faster and faster until water splashed. Ruby pulled the animal back before he had her drenched.

Carson walked out the door of the stable and joined her. He looked her horse over. "Is he fresh enough for a ride?"

"Now?" She glanced at her watch.

"Why not? Do you have somewhere you have to be?"

"Yes, actually, I do. I have to go home and fix dinner for my family."

He stood on the opposite side of her horse, leaning on the saddle to watch her, as if he knew she was looking for ways to get out of spending time with him. And he wasn't giving her an inch of wiggle room.

"You could invite me to dinner," he suggested.

"No. Carson, this isn't going to happen."

"A ride isn't going to happen? Or dinner?"

"No, this." She pointed from him to herself and back to him. "We are not going to happen."

"Right, of course we aren't." He walked around her horse and was suddenly at her side. "I'm asking you to go for a ride. An hour or two of relaxation, not worrying about the thefts, your brother, Iva, Brandon and all of the other stuff piling up on us. I could use that break."

She closed her eyes and prayed for strength. He was her kryptonite, it seemed, because she had no strength. "Carson."

When she opened her eyes, he was still in front of her, his smile a little bit sweet and a little bit rakish. "Yes?"

"Why are you doing this?"

"Simple. We have unfinished business, Ruby. You left and I've spent a lot of years wondering why."

"Because I wasn't good for you," she whispered. "We were young and making decisions that would have…"

"Changed everything?" he asked. "Because I've thought about that a lot over the years. My life would have been different if you'd been in it."

"Mine, too," she admitted, trying to look away from him. His fingers touched her chin, drawing her back to him, forcing her gaze to meet his.

"You could have moved on." His tone made it sound as if the words came easily to him, but she could hear the heavy thread of emotion in his voice. "You didn't."

"No, I didn't. And neither did you."

He shrugged that off. "I was wrong once. I didn't want to be wrong again."

"Wrong?"

"About us." He walked away, ending the moment. "I'll saddle a horse."

"But I—" She tried to drag her horse to the door that he'd disappeared through. The crazy animal wouldn't be pulled away from the water. "Carson!"

He looked around the corner of the door, one side of his mouth tipped in a grin. "Yes?"

Objections. She had some. She had a few. But looking at him, she couldn't seem to get them out. Instead, she shook her head.

"Never mind."

"Good. That's what I was hoping."

He returned a few minutes later with a pretty roan mare. Ruby instantly loved the horse with its sweet face and warm eyes. She thought horses were a lot like people; their eyes revealed so much about their personality. This one was a keeper.

."Like her?" Carson asked as he tightened the cinch.

"She's really nice." She took a step closer and this time her gelding left the water that he'd been playing in.

"You can ride her," he offered, handing her the reins.

"No. Dusty is fine." She ran a hand down her horse's neck, drawing him close. She wouldn't want him to feel bad.

"Come on, you know you want to."

Yes, she did. She looked up at the man who fairly towered over her and she felt...not overpowered, not at all. She felt safe. He held the reins out again and she took them.

"Thank you." She stepped close to the horse and too close to Carson.

They both stilled. The horses moved restlessly, swishing tails to brush away flies. Dusty pulled his head back to the water trough. Such a bad habit, Ruby thought. She had to break him of that.

She had to break herself of some bad habits, too. Starting with Carson Thorn. Unfortunately, he was a habit she really didn't want to break. Being hundreds of miles away she'd really thought she'd managed to get over him. Now, being close again, she realized that maybe she'd never stopped loving him.

The word froze in her mind, and she quickly stepped away, making a big deal about checking the stirrups before mounting. She couldn't love a man who could so easily forget her. A man who had to know that if she hadn't taken his father's money, it was because she'd loved him more than any amount James Thorn could have written on a check.

She loved him. And the past was between them in a way that she wasn't sure she could forget. She would never be able to forget his dad standing on her front porch with that check or the humiliation burning her cheeks when he'd told her she needed to let Carson be somebody. His son could be a senator. He could be anything. But not with the daughter of Earl Donovan at his side.

The memories were burned into her mind. Branded.

They rode side by side. Ruby had gone quiet since they'd left. Carson knew eventually she'd talk, so he didn't push. Instead, he relaxed. He relaxed and he enjoyed the breeze sweeping down the hillside, swirling the autumn grass and cooling the air.

"You're right," she finally spoke. "This is nice."

"How do you like the mare?"

"She's as sweet to ride as she is to look at. Where did you get her?"

"She's out of my old mare."

"I should have known."

Yes, she should have. She'd always loved that mare. Years ago he'd considered giving her the horse. A pretty dappled gray that he'd hauled to her place and let her ride.

"I've been offered a job," he told her out of the blue, surprising himself with the announcement.

She glanced his way, her eyes widening. "You have a job. Two of them, if I'm not mistaken."

He pushed his hat back just a smidge to get a better look at the woman riding next to him. It did take him back, this ride, her next to him. The years seemed to melt away.

"State Department of Agriculture."

"Politics," she murmured. She looked away.

"Don't say it like it's poison." He nearly laughed. "I didn't say I was going to take it. I do have to admit, there are times I would like to try something different. I've been ranching my whole life."

"Your dad wanted you to be a senator," she said so softly he almost missed it.

"Yes, he did. He had a lot of plans for my

life." He rode his horse a little closer to hers. "Ruby?"

She cleared her throat. "Let's talk about something else. Or maybe not talk at all."

They rode a little farther in the direction of the hills and the spring. They wouldn't make it there, not today. The temperature had dropped an easy ten degrees and clouds were rolling in from the south. Ruby shot him a worried look.

"Do you have radar on your phone?" she asked as they reined in their horses.

"Yeah, give me a sec. I'm not sure how much signal we have out here."

"Probably not a lot."

He had his phone out, but a look up at the increasingly dark clouds told him a lot more than the app that wouldn't load on his phone. As he studied the clouds, Ruby moved her horse closer to his. She touched his arm and when he looked at her, she pointed to a distant service road that ran along the boundary of his property.

A truck, covered in mud, pulled a rusted-out trailer.

"Someone you know?" she asked.

"No, and I doubt the Jensens are out moving cattle in this weather. That's their property on the other side of the road."

"Should we try to catch up and see who it

is?" Ruby had already nudged her horse forward. Carson rode up next to her.

"We can try, but I think they'll be gone before we get there."

Ruby shot him a look that called him chicken. "I'm going."

And with that she was off. He urged the gelding forward, knowing the roan she was riding would give them a run for their money.

"Hey, remember the gully." He yelled the warning as she streaked across the field.

"I remember." Her words floated back to him.

Carson grinned, watching as she raced across the field, her free hand pushing down the hat that threatened to lift off her head.

As they closed in on the service road the truck sped up. It must have seen them. They reached the gully with Ruby a short distance ahead of him. She leaned over the horse's neck and the two of them flew across the narrow ditch. His horse stumbled a bit but got its footing.

Ahead of him, Ruby slowed her horse and turned to watch him catch up. Her dimple flashed and her eyes sparkled. He wanted to snatch that hat off her head and release the auburn hair, knowing it would fall around her shoulders, silky and scented of something herbal.

Her lips parted and his attention refocused, from her hair to her mouth. Because her mouth, he knew how it would taste. Dangerous thoughts, he warned himself. Dangerous distraction. He turned back to the road and the truck that was disappearing from sight. His phone was useless out here, so he couldn't call anyone, and the truck was too far away for a clear picture. At least he could give Lucy a somewhat decent description of the old Ford and the rusted-out trailer.

Thunder rumbled overhead and the horses started to shift, ears twitching. He didn't need to look up to know they were in serious trouble. They were a good thirty-minute ride from the house, even at a run. The wind had picked up and the sky was about to open up on them.

"The old hunting shack," he called out over the blowing wind. "Remember?"

She nodded and turned her horse in the direction of the trees. The going was rough as the terrain became rocky and a lot less than level leading to the hill area. The rain had started to come down and wind whipped at them from all directions.

The shack was situated in the woods at the base of the hills. It took them a few minutes to reach it. When they did, they were soaked. The horses were soaked. They made their way to the lean-to on the side of the building and tied the horses in the small enclosure. A door led into the shack from the lean-to. Carson pushed it open and peeked in, not sure what they'd find inside. It had been years since anyone had used it for hunting.

Ruby slid in next to him. He drew her in, his arm around her. The place was dusty with cobwebs. From the nest of leaves, twigs and trash, it looked as if some kind of varmint called it home. Carson looked around, making sure the four-legged inhabitant wasn't lurking under the cot or the wood stove.

"What do we do now?" Ruby shivered, standing in front of a stove that hadn't held a fire in probably ten years.

"I guess we wait this out. I'll call Ben and tell him where we are. Do you have your phone?"

"No signal at all."

"I've got a signal. Barely. I'll call Iva for you."

She nodded, still shivering, hugging herself for warmth. "Thank you. And do you think we should call Lucy and tell her about that truck and trailer?"

"I'll make that the first call."

He made the calls. Ruby walked out the side

door, leaving him alone. She came back a few minutes later with some old pieces of wood and even a piece of rail from a wood fence.

He pocketed his phone. "I made the calls. Where did you find that?"

"Against the side of the building, under the roof. There's a little more. Enough to make a fire, but it won't last long."

"You realize we don't have matches."

She groaned as she dropped the wood next to the stove. "We'd never make it on a reality show."

"Probably not." He went to a cabinet and shoved through some leftover items from the last hunting trip he'd taken with his dad. Some rusted-out cans of soup, a container of coffee that had been gnawed on. He moved a few things and found what he was looking for. "Eureka, matches."

When he turned, she was standing behind him, goose bumps on her arms and her hair dripping water. He brushed the wet hair back from her face, and she closed her eyes, lashes fanning dark against her fair skin. Forgetting matches, forgetting the fire, he wrapped her in his arms and pulled her close.

She shivered against him but she nestled her head against his shoulder, her arms going around his waist. He inhaled the scent of her hair, damp skin and rain and held her tight.

"This is better," she whispered against him.

He couldn't have agreed more. His lips brushed the top of her head. She looked up and when she did, he leaned, brushing his lips across hers. He knew he shouldn't. She probably had the same thought. Better not to go there.

But a dozen years without her in his life felt like walking across the widest desert with no water in sight.

She moved her arms from around him and raised her hands to touch his cheeks, and then her fingers were in his hair. And he was lost. He whispered her name against her cheek and then his lips claimed hers again.

He'd kissed her years ago, the way a boy kissed a girl. They had been young, discovering love and attraction, all of the things that happened to teenagers. Today he kissed the woman and it rocked his world. He kissed her because it was right, and it had never been right with anyone else. He'd never felt a need to hold a woman forever the way he wanted to hold her.

A crash of thunder shook the little shack, and wind beat against the thin panes of glass in the windows. As the storm rolled through,

Carson rediscovered the reason he wanted only this one woman. Because she was the other half of him.

Eventually she pulled away, shaken, her cheeks flushed with color. "Carson, I…"

"Don't regret," he warned.

"No, I don't regret. I'm just not sure what we're doing. Or what we're going to do."

"Do we have to answer those questions right now?" He pulled her against him. "I need you in my life."

"And I needed you twelve years ago."

He cupped her cheeks with his hands and kissed her again. "I can't undo what my dad did. I can't undo any of that. But I know what I want."

"I don't know."

"Really?" He stepped back from her, brushing a hand across his face. "I'm not sure what that means."

"I don't think we can just sweep it all under the rug. We can't sweep the past under a rug and we can't pretend that everyone in town, including you, hasn't suspected my brother of being a cattle thief. We also can't pretend that I fit in your world."

"Okay, so we talk about the past and we figure out how to keep Derek from suspicion."

"That sounds so easy," she whispered. "I

want it to be that easy. Let's just forget, pretend none of it matters and move on. But you're not wired like that and neither am I. We both have a lot of stuff to deal with. Not just the past and Derek, but now you have Brandon to consider. I have Iva and her health."

"Those aren't obstacles."

"They are," she insisted with a sadness to her voice that shook him. "They are my obstacles. I have to keep them safe."

"I know you do." He didn't reach for her. Any man with half a brain would know that it was the wrong time for that. She was holding on by a string and she didn't want to cry.

He backed up to one of the old rocking chairs and sat down. She took the other and moved it to face him. The rain against the metal roof had slowed from pounding to a rhythmic beat that almost soothed. The shack grew quiet in the calm after the storm.

"We should go." She looked at her watch as she said it. "I really do need to go."

"I know you do. Give it a few minutes to blow over and we'll head out."

She nodded and then drew her knees up, wrapping her arms around them. Her eyes closed.

She was right. Where did they go from here? He had no idea. But it was obvious that they'd left a lot undone and unsaid.

Chapter Eleven

Ruby walked up the steps to her grandmother's house, weary to the bone, still damp from the rain and ready for a warm bath. But as she walked through the front door she was met with chaos.

Her grandmother looked up from her recliner, her poor body jerking as she tried to point at Derek who stood next to her.

"Tell him I will not go." Iva shook her head and sighed. "I won't go to the hospital."

"What's going on?" Ruby hurried to her grandmother's side. "I shouldn't have left you. I should—"

Iva held up a hand that jerked but she steadied it and she frowned big. "You have to take time off. So, yes, you should have gone. You deserve—"

It was Ruby's turn to stop her grandmother.

"Don't say it. If you are going to say something about Carson and myself, please don't."

Derek bristled. She looked up at her little brother. He looked angry. She didn't want his anger on top of her own, on top of her grandmother's deteriorating health.

"I had a good ride. It rained. I'm home. And Gran, you have to rest. I'm going to take a guess. You've been up all day cooking? Cleaning? What else? Who have you been taking care of?"

"We have neighbors who are sick. I made a dinner and had Derek take it to Janie Douglas because Howard had a heart attack."

"Of course you did. But it would really be okay if you let someone else take a meal. Let someone else visit church members in the hospital."

Iva shook her head. "Oh, Ruby, you know they won't. You know that people don't think about their neighbors anymore. Everyone is busy. Too busy to visit a sick church member. Too busy to take a meal."

Ruby sat on a nearby chair. "I know."

"So, I have to do it."

She didn't argue. She knew she would lose. "Okay, we can have a compromise. You can do all of these things, but not all on the same day. And when you're tired, rest."

"She should go to the ER." Derek looked a little worn out himself, but he also looked determined.

"I think she just needs to rest. But if she needs to go, she'll be honest and tell us." Ruby stood, smiling down at her grandmother. "We should eat something."

Her grandmother smiled. "I made soup."

Ruby leaned to kiss her grandmother's cheek. "Of course you did."

She started to walk away, but Iva stopped her. "So how is Carson?"

"He's just fine."

Outside a horn honked. Derek looked startled as he glanced at his watch. "Oh, man, I'm late."

"Late for what?" Ruby walked to the window, pushed back the curtain and looked out. The red convertible and a pretty blonde.

"I have a date," he admitted.

Ruby looked back at her brother, surprised by the red in his cheeks. "Tell her to come in and meet us. I doubt Gran would put up with a guy honking for me. I don't see why it's any different for a girl to honk and a guy to go running."

"It isn't," Iva said with a grin. "Let's meet this girl who has you wearing cologne."

"No."

"Why not?" Ruby asked.

"Because, Ruby. I'm not having her come in here."

That did it. Ruby shot her brother an angry glare and headed for the door. "Derek, she can either come in and meet your family or she can admit now that she thinks she's too good for you. Or do you think you're not good enough?"

"Ruby," Iva warned. "This isn't the same."

At that Ruby turned to look at her grandmother. "It is the same. She's sitting out there in a car that would cost more than this house, sunglasses that cost more than my entire wardrobe and she won't walk up the front steps and meet his family. Or he doesn't want her to meet us."

Derek was at her side, his eyes narrowing. "Calm down. I'll go get her. But I'm not sixteen and you're not my mother." He paused. "And this isn't about you."

That unsettled her. "I'm sorry. I don't know what's wrong with me."

"Maybe the guy pulling up the drive has something to do with that. You'd better not go running if he honks." Derek half grinned at his warning as he walked out the door.

"What's Carson doing here?" Ruby spun to face her grandmother, remembering the homemade soup in the kitchen. A clue. She should have paid attention to the clues.

"When he called to tell me you all were stuck in that cabin, I told him to bring Brandon over for soup."

"You shouldn't have."

Iva gave her a pointed look. "Really?"

The conversation had nowhere to go. Besides that, Brandon was heading at a fast pace for the front door. Behind him, Carson called out for him to wait. And Derek was opening the car door for his girlfriend, who looked just as shiny and pretty as her car. Ruby looked down at her own rain-soaked clothes and tried to avoid her reflection in the glass of the storm door because she knew her hair hung limp around her face. She probably had streaks of mascara running down her cheeks.

On the other side of the door, Brandon waited, a big grin on his face. She pushed the door open and let the little boy in. She reminded herself that insecurity wasn't an attractive trait. She'd put herself through college. She'd worked her way up in the state of Oklahoma as a supervisor for family services. She was educated, knew how to handle juveniles, angry parents and state officials.

It was time to stop thinking she wasn't good enough. Only one person, no two, had ever made her feel that way. Both were related to Carson. His father and his sister.

Only two people. She had to stop letting those two people, the memory of what they'd done, control her thoughts about herself.

She was more.

She faced Carson with that thought in mind. "Carson."

"Surprise," he said as he walked through the door she opened for him. He had changed into jeans, a buttoned-up shirt and boots that a man didn't wear to work on a farm. Her eyes soaked up the sight of him. "I would have told you, but I had a feeling you'd uninvite us. And I do love Iva's homemade soup."

"Of course you do." She glanced past him at Derek and the girl, now standing outside her car, their arms around each other.

"Alyssa Meadows," Carson said. "Her dad has a big spread about twenty miles from here."

"I've never heard of them."

Carson glanced back at the young couple. "They sold out in California and moved here a few years ago. She's a decent girl. She looks high maintenance, but I've been over there and seen her working cattle right along with her dad and brothers."

Ruby nodded, willing to let it go.

When she turned from the window, Brandon was helping Iva to her feet, her unsteady hands on the walker. It hurt to see her struggle this way. The hurt deepened knowing that in a matter of months she would be in a wheelchair. In Ruby's sporadic trips home over the past few years, Iva had managed to keep the disease a secret. This past summer when Ruby visited, it had been obvious. There had been a rapid progression since her visit at Christmas.

"Gran, take a seat at the dining-room table. You cooked. I'll serve." Ruby walked next to her grandmother as they made slow progress from living room to dining room.

"I think I'll take you up on that offer," Iva said, even her voice shaking as her body weakened. "Not because I have to."

"No, of course not." Ruby leaned to kiss her grandmother's powdered cheek. She pulled out a chair, and Iva sat with a sigh of relief.

She heard the front door open, then heard Derek saying something about they wouldn't stay long. Ruby and Iva exchanged a look.

A few minutes later Derek had entered the room with the woman, Alyssa. She was pretty, but not overwhelming. There was something fragile about her, something that made her more likable. Derek, all brash confidence and cowboy tough, softened in her presence. His hand was laced through hers and he looked down at her as if she might be the best thing ever.

"Ruby, Gran, this is Alyssa Meadows. Alyssa, this is my family. And our neighbors, Carson Thorn and his nephew, Brandon." He looked at Alyssa as he spoke, saying the words clearly, and Alyssa watched him speaking to her.

After the introduction Alyssa held out a hand for Ruby to shake. "Ruby, I've heard so much about you."

The young woman spoke, but her words were low and not easily understood. Ruby didn't glance at her brother but she knew if she did look at him, his features would be hard with that protective streak of his. Alyssa Meadows was deaf.

"It's nice to finally meet you, Alyssa." Taking her cue from Derek, Ruby made eye contact with the younger woman and spoke clearly.

And she meant it. It was good to meet Alyssa. Her brother had changed. Maybe this young woman had something to do with those changes.

Ruby's gaze dropped to a pretty sapphire necklace hanging from Alyssa's neck. "That's a beautiful necklace."

"Derek bought it for me. For my birthday." Alyssa smiled up at Derek.

"That was sweet of him." This time she did look at her brother. And he didn't look guilty or as if anything was out of place. But the necklace? How had he bought something that expensive? She hated that her first thoughts were to suspect him of something criminal.

"Are we going to eat?" Brandon appeared at her side, a big grin on his face. "Iva told me to ask. And Uncle Carson is getting bowls."

"Of course he is," she said. She ruffled her fingers through the little boy's hair. "I'll help him."

She looked around the dining room, filled to overflowing with people. Filled with laughter and conversation.

And then she looked toward her kitchen, filled with Carson Thorn's presence. She watched as he moved around the tiny space, totally at ease. He had bowls of soup on the counter and he had put rolls in a basket.

"Making yourself at home, aren't you?" She stopped next to him at the counter.

"I thought I'd make myself useful," he admitted as he dished soup into a bowl. "Iva always made me feel welcomed this way."

"Yes, she did. From the first, when Dad… when he died and she brought us here, it felt like home. It felt safe." Even after all of these years it stung. The tears blurred her vision and she had to inhale to keep it together. Her dad had done his best. She'd always known that. He'd been a man left alone with two kids and a dream. He'd missed the woman who had been his anchor.

He'd expected Ruby to become his anchor. And she'd done her best.

"Yeah, I'm sure it did." Carson turned from the bowls of soup and his gaze turned her inside out. "Iva knows how to take care of people."

They'd had this conversation before, years ago. She'd told him about those few years when they lived in the pull-behind RV, sometimes settling for a month or two in one place, never going to school. Her dad had bought them textbooks and it had been up to her to make sure they did schoolwork. Cooking had been up to her. Raising Derek, also up to her.

When Iva had taken them in, she'd worked hard to make Ruby let go of that need to parent, to take charge. She'd insisted that Ruby be a child.

As a social worker, Ruby had seen too many kids like herself, used to being the adult. And in each of those cases she'd urged the foster parents to do as Iva had done, make sure the children became children again.

"We should feed them before this gets cold,"

she said, picking up two bowls and heading for the dining room.

Carson followed her.

They carried bowls of soup to the dining room. Ruby paused midstep when she saw her brother using sign language, smiling as he spoke to Alyssa. The young woman's hands flew and her face beamed.

Who was this young man her brother was becoming? Ruby felt a bit of pride watching him, seeing the changes that were taking place. He was becoming a man.

She had to let him grow up. She couldn't protect him. She couldn't make decisions for him.

"He's good," Carson whispered behind her. "She's good for him."

She nodded and placed bowls of soup on the table before turning to go back for more. Carson followed her. It might have been better if he hadn't. He could sit down, give her space and she could finish bringing the food to the table. But no, she didn't get that break. He followed her to the kitchen, standing close behind her as she finished gathering bowls. He picked up the basket of rolls.

"You smell like rain," he said as they walked out of the kitchen.

She shot him a look and saw that he was

smirking just a bit. "Thank you. I feel like a drowned rat, so it's good to know I smell like one, too. You're very charming."

He laughed at that. "Now you're putting words in my mouth. I've said nothing about rats. You look fresh and beautiful. And that's what I mean. Rain is—" he paused, leaning closer "—good."

"Right." She slipped away from him because the air in the kitchen seemed heavy and hard to breathe. "We should eat. I'm starving."

"I'm starving, too."

She ignored him. She ignored the painful thud of her heart against her ribs. She definitely ignored the knowing look Iva shot her as they sat down at the table side by side.

After they'd cleared the table and washed the dishes, Ruby walked Carson and Brandon out to his truck. He guessed she wasn't going to invite him to stay for a cup of coffee. He smiled at that thought. He hadn't expected that offer, not after he'd blindsided her by showing up for dinner. He guessed he should have told her back at the shack. He lifted Brandon into the backseat of the truck. The little boy leaned to whisper and Carson laughed and stepped back after the boy asked his question.

"He wants you to buckle him in."

Ruby stepped forward. "I think I can do that."

She reached to pull the seat belt over the little boy in his booster seat. He was sleepy and wrapped his arms around her neck. Carson, leaning against the open door, watched.

"I love you, Ruby." Brandon, only five, but a boy with game. He got the goodbye hug that Carson doubted he'd get. Ruby kissed the little boy and hugged him good-night.

"I love you, too. Now go home and get a good night's sleep."

Carson closed the door, peering through the window at the little boy who was in his life for who knew how long. A few weeks ago he'd been alone in a big, rambling house. He'd been responsible for the ranch and himself. He hadn't known how quickly life could change.

He turned to face the woman, the other change, a welcome change in his life.

"I should get him home and into bed." He took a step toward her, not willing to take that chance that she'd rebuff a kiss good-night, but wanting to kiss her good-night.

They'd been in this yard before, standing under this same moon, these same stars.

"I need to go in and help Gran get ready for bed." She stepped back from him. "Have you had any progress with the lawyer?"

He glanced inside the truck at the little guy

almost asleep now. "Yeah, he thinks I have a good case and that I'll get guardianship."

"I'm sorry. That can't be easy."

"No, it isn't easy," he admitted as he reached to open the truck door. "I'll see you soon?"

"I'm not sure, I—"

"Don't think of excuses."

"Not excuses," she insisted. "It's just that this is too easy, Carson. We can't pretend there aren't unresolved issues between us."

"Then let's talk it out."

She touched his face, her palm cool against his cheek. And then she backed away, dropping her hand to her side.

Yeah, it was definitely time to go. "We'll talk more tomorrow."

She shook her head. "Gran has an appointment in Austin."

"Do you need Derek? He's working for me tomorrow, but I can turn him loose if you're going to need help."

"No, I won't need him. Is he doing okay at your place? I appreciate you giving him the hours."

"He's a good worker, Ruby. I can put him on a job and he stays with it until it's finished."

"And if he's busy at your place, he isn't a suspect. I hope."

He didn't know what to say to that. She must

have seen it in his expression because she gave him a cautious look.

"Is he still a suspect, Carson?"

"There are people around town who are still pointing fingers. That's going to happen until we catch the thieves."

"I understand that. I guess what I need to know is do *you* think he's a suspect?"

"I don't think he's a suspect."

She stood on tiptoe and kissed his cheek. "Thank you. And good night."

Yes, good-night. He got in his truck and headed back to his place. Brandon slept in the backseat. The little boy stayed asleep when Carson got him out of the truck and carried him inside and upstairs to the bedroom next to Carson's.

He woke up as Carson tucked him in, pulling the blanket up to his chin. "Is my mom back?"

Carson sat down on the edge of the bed, surprised by the question. "No, kiddo, she isn't back. Why do you ask that?"

Beneath the blanket the little boy shrugged. "I had a dream. Do you think she's coming back?"

What did he say to that question? Brandon watched him, dark eyes sleepy and serious, as he waited for an answer.

"I think she will. But I don't know when.

But we'll make it together until she does, right? You and me?"

Brandon nodded but tears filled his eyes, and that was almost too much for Carson. He placed a hand on his nephew's shoulder.

A sniffle and then a little hand brushed at his eyes. Brandon nodded once and managed to look like a little boy who wasn't going to cry. "Yeah, you and me."

"I'm sorry, kiddo. I know this is tough. I'm not much of a cook. And I don't know many stories."

"But you take me to Ruby's and she teaches me to ride. I can be a rancher someday. And Derek says I'm mighty good at roping."

"I think you'll definitely be a rancher. And a mighty good calf roper in time."

"Can I have my own horse?"

Carson patted his shoulder. "Soon."

Brandon yawned and rubbed his eyes again. "Okay. I'm going to sleep now. If my mom calls, will you tell her I miss her?"

"I promise to tell her you miss her. And I bet she misses you, too."

"Yeah, she always misses me."

That stopped him. Carson watched his nephew, not wanting to push, but not willing to let this go. "When does she miss you?"

"When she leaves me with her friend Amy."

"Does she do that a lot?"

"Just sometimes. Good night, Uncle Carson."

"Good night, Brandon. I love you."

Brandon closed his eyes but he smiled. "I love you, too. And I like Ruby a lot."

"Yeah, me, too."

He kissed his nephew on the forehead and then got up and walked to the door. He stood there for a long minute, watching his nephew drift off to sleep, curled on his side with a stuffed bear. Because guys could have bears and not be a sissy, he'd told Carson. Once he was sure Brandon was asleep, Carson flipped off the light and walked back downstairs.

For five years he'd lived in this house alone. He'd accepted his solitary existence. He'd pretended that memories of Ruby never made him wonder what they might have been like, if things had been different. If she hadn't left.

He walked to his office and unlocked the safe. Tucked at the back of the box was a gift he'd never gotten a chance to give. He pulled it out and lifted the lid, exposing the engagement ring to the light of day for the first time in years. The diamond twinkled in the overhead light. The platinum gleamed as if it hadn't been years.

If things had been different, he would have proposed that summer when he'd returned home from college. He'd planned it all out. The restaurant, the words, the promises. When he'd gotten home, she'd been gone. She'd taken his dad's money and moved to Oklahoma where she planned to go to college.

He'd thought about going after her. He'd wanted to know why the money had been more important than their relationship. Wounded pride had kept him from going, kept him from asking. And in all of the years in between, when he'd known she was home visiting, he hadn't approached her. He'd never bothered to ask Iva. Iva had never volunteered anything, other than to say the two of them should talk.

The years had hardened his heart. His pride had gotten in the way, convincing him he didn't need her. His faith, the faith his mother had raised him to trust in, had crumbled until he'd become one of those people who did little more than say they believed in God.

The ranch had become everything. It was his life. He ate, slept and breathed ranching.

Until this month when a little boy had crashed into his life and Ruby had showed back up. But where did he go from here? He put the lid back on the box and placed the ring back in the safe where it had been for twelve years.

Chapter Twelve

The weather had turned cool. The third week in October should have still been warm. Instead, a cool front had settled over the area. He'd gone from T-shirts to long-sleeve flannel shirts. As he walked into the league building on Tuesday he couldn't avoid Ingrid and her cinnamon rolls. She practically ran him down, holding the plate out with one hand and pushing her glasses up with the other.

"I made these last night," she said it with a big smile splitting her face. He had to admit, they did smell pretty good.

"Don't mind if I do." He grabbed one off the plate. "It won't be long, Ingrid, and some man is going to snatch you up, and you won't have time to bake for the rest of us."

"Thanks, Carson. I keep hoping. I joined a singles group at a church I've been going to."

"That sounds like the best place for you to meet someone. Don't you still go to Little Horn Community?"

She laughed at that. "Carson, you need to go to church. I haven't been there in ages."

"You're right, I do need to go. And thanks for breakfast. I'm going to pour myself a cup of coffee and eat this roll before the rest of the members get here."

She nodded, indicating past his right shoulder. "Ben is already here. So is Byron. They have a letter from Iva Donovan."

"Resigning?"

"Yeah, I'm afraid so. Is it because everyone is being so hard on Derek?"

"No, she's just not able. Her health isn't good."

Ingrid pulled a frown that was genuine and sympathetic. "I'm real sorry to hear that. I can't imagine this place without Iva here. But I bet you're real happy to have Ruby back in town."

He opened his mouth, unsure of what to say, and figured he probably looked like a fish gasping for air. Or whatever a fish gasped for. "Well, I know Iva is glad she's back in town."

"Of course she is." With that, Ingrid headed back to her desk, not really hiding her soft laughter.

Thirty minutes later the meeting came to

order and within minutes the whole mess of them was arguing, coming up with suspects and generally causing chaos. Carson sat down in his chair and looked at them. Grown men and women fighting like kids on a playground.

"Could I call this meeting to order?" he said with the enthusiasm of a man about to get a root canal. "Or could I just go and let the whole bunch of you fight it out?"

Ben, leaning back in the chair next to Carson's, laughed at that. He ran a hand through his hair and grinned as he looked at the others gathered around the table. "Well, I guess you could pick up that gavel and knock a few heads. Maybe that would get their attention."

Carson slammed the gavel on the table and sudden silence fell on the room. Ben crossed his arms over his chest and chuckled. The others looked at him.

"I would really like to call this meeting to order. Maybe the rest of you have all day. I have work to do," he said. *And a kid at home.*

Brandon would be at the house by now. He was safe with the housekeeper, but that didn't mean he wouldn't want Carson home to hang out with. Carson had realized that with a five-year-old in the house, he spent a little less time working these days.

"I guess we have Iva's resignation from the board?" Byron McKay asked.

Ingrid handed him the letter. Byron looked it over, shook his head and shoved it back in the envelope. "I hate to see that."

"We all do. We'll have to fill her position when we have our monthly session of all members of the league." Carson looked over his notes. "Lucy was going to be here, but she's at the Garveys', looking at tire tracks to see if they match others that we've found."

Lynette Fields looked up from her cell phone. "The Garveys lost a dozen head. And then there was the Jensens' and that truck you saw out here. They didn't lose cattle, but someone took equipment from a garage."

"Lucy has an itemized list at the police station," Ben offered, leaning forward and putting all four legs of his chair back on the floor. "Does anyone have any idea who that truck and trailer might belong to?"

Byron smirked at that. "Well, if we did, Ben, I guess we'd have this little crime spree brought to an end, wouldn't we?"

"Byron, one of these days someone is going to—"

Carson banged his gavel and gave Ben a look. "What else did Lucy have to say?"

Ben shrugged, but there was an odd glint

in his eyes. "I can't rightly remember. I think she said something like, 'Ben Stillwater, get out of my office before I arrest you for being so stinking charming.'"

A few snickers followed his statement. Carson knew if he didn't get the meeting back on track it would derail, and they wouldn't accomplish anything. He had a lot to accomplish.

"I'd like to make a suggestion." He cleared his throat to get the attention of the members present. "We have two scholarships a year and a few job placements. I'm going to offer Derek Donovan an apprenticeship. He's good with horses, and I'd like to see him work with my show horses."

"That's your problem," Byron McKay grumbled from the other end of the table. "Hire him or don't. It's your livestock that will come up missing."

"Byron, you can't keep pointing fingers at people who aren't suspects."

"I guess you haven't seen that necklace the Meadows girl is wearing. How'd he buy that?"

"I guess he saved up the money," Carson said. He pushed two fingers against his pounding temples and shook his head. "I've had enough of this. Iva isn't the only one ready to resign."

"Maybe you're just looking for a way out

so you can take that government job." Byron, once again.

Carson shot him a look. "Let's get back to business. I'd like to nominate Derek as a candidate for a scholarship."

"On what grounds?" Lynette asked.

"On the grounds that he's working hard to improve his life. He shows a real aptitude and he could use a hand."

Byron came out of his chair. "We're not a charity organization. Leave that to Miss Klondike and let the rest of us get back to ranching."

Amelia Klondike turned a few shades of pink and brushed a hand through her blond hair, but she didn't cow down to Byron's thundering words. Instead, she met him head on. "Byron, I'm not sure why you think helping a man better himself is charity."

"Because I think we're feeding Derek Donovan twice. He's stealing our cattle, and now we're going to give him a job."

"I think we should all think about this," Lynette offered. The voice of reason. "Derek made a mistake a couple of years ago and he's paid for that mistake. Now we have the opportunity to help him become a man who can support himself, and I think we should meet again next week to vote."

Byron stood, all bluster and self-importance. "I vote no."

"Of course you do," Ben said to the older man's back as he went out the door.

The members who remained finished the meeting. As they were wrapping up things, Carson's phone rang. He excused himself to answer and walked out of the office. He kept walking to the front door and then outside, pulling on his hat as he went.

"Jenna. So you haven't fallen off the face of the earth." He wanted to have compassion, but it got tangled up with temper because he thought of her little boy asking him if his mom was coming back.

"No, I haven't. I want to come home." Her voice sounded shaky.

Carson headed down the sidewalk, the phone to his ear. "I don't see anyone stopping you."

"Is Brandon okay?"

Deep breath. Carson inhaled and shoved his hat down, trying hard to remember this was his sister. "Yeah, thanks for asking."

And then she started to cry. Of course she did. He was trying hard to hang on to being mad, because anger would keep him from falling for lies. When she started to cry, it chipped away at that anger.

"I love him," she sobbed.

"I know you do."

She sniffled. "I'm not good at doing this alone. Since Jeff left me, it's been hard to focus."

Okay, that helped him get back on track. "Jenna, you have to focus. You have a son and he needs you. He needs you here with him. He needs a mom."

"I know that better than anyone, Carson."

The need for a mom. He let out a sigh. "Jenna, life isn't fair. I'm sorry that you felt alone."

"We're pretty dysfunctional, aren't we?" she said.

"Don't include me in your drama." He paced, trying to avoid people walking down the sidewalk shooting him curious looks, trying to overhear.

"You're not perfect."

"No, I'm not. But this isn't about me. Brandon needs for you to come home and stay home. No more walking away. Come home and we'll get help here. Whatever you need." He shifted the phone to the other hand, the other ear. His gaze got caught on a car pulling up to the post office.

He watched as Ruby got out, all cowgirl in faded jeans, a T-shirt and a white hat.

"Carson, I do want to come home. But I need a job and a way to take care of Brandon."

"That's something we'll talk about."

"What do you mean?" she asked. "Carson, he's my son."

"The boy that you randomly leave with me and with Amy? Who else do you leave him with?"

"I don't leave him with strangers if that's what you mean."

"You're a twenty-seven-year-old woman who has a child. You've been married twice. You haven't held down a job or kept a place to live in, not since you left home and left college."

"Okay…" Her voice drifted off. He didn't want her defeated. He wanted her to accept her mistakes and grow up.

He told her that. "Jenna, for your son, you have to make better choices. Come home. You can live in the house on the twenty across the road. But you can't have Brandon. I'm going to get guardianship and you're going to allow that."

"For good?"

"No, just until you prove to me you can hold it together and be a mom." He glanced both ways and headed across the street. "I have to go."

"So I can come home?"

"Of course you can come home. Jenna, we want you here."

"I want to come home."

"Brandon will be glad. I'll be glad when you're here. We'll figure this out."

The call ended. He slipped the phone in his pocket and headed for the post office. As he headed that way he realized his mistake. Ruby had been joined by Amelia Klondike, Eva Brooks and Sheriff Lucy Benson. Great.

Ruby had met up with Lucy Benson in the post office. The two had talked about life in the small town of Little Horn, and then they discussed the truck and trailer Ruby and Carson had seen on the service road at the edge of his property. And Lucy had apologized for searching the Donovan place. As the two walked outside, Amelia Klondike, coming out of the Lone Star Cowboy League headquarters, waved and headed their way. Ruby liked Amelia. She was old money and class, but she had a big heart and loved everyone.

"Hey, you all want to have pie at Maggie's?" Amelia called out.

Lucy glanced at her watch. "I've got to head to the office and brief my officer coming on duty. But I'd love a rain check."

As they talked, Eva Brooks, Ben Stillwater's cousin, got out of her car. She waved and headed their way.

This was what Ruby loved and had missed about small towns. She had missed knowing people. She'd missed standing on the sidewalk having a heart-to-heart with people she'd known her whole life.

"Amelia, what about the electric bill for the Barlow ranch?" Lucy asked as they moved to the side for a couple walking down the sidewalk.

"It wasn't me, or the Here to Help group, Lucy. I'd love to take credit for everything happening in this town, but I'm just one person and a great committee. We really aren't behind all of the benevolence going on around here. Would you like me to give you a list of what we've done and plan to do in the next couple of weeks? Until this ends I wouldn't mind giving you our monthly reports."

"That would help," Lucy said. "I'm sorry to put that much extra work on you, but if we have a list we don't have to question. We'll know who is getting what, and if something extra happens, we'll know to do some research. I really dislike having to question good deeds. It makes me feel a little sick."

Eva touched her arm. The pretty redhead

was naturally warm and friendly. Ruby didn't know her that well, but she liked her.

"Don't worry about it. We all understand. If people don't understand, then that's a problem they have."

Lucy's gaze settled on Ruby. "Yes, but sometimes I have to question a friend. That's a part of the job I don't like. And speaking of my job, I have to go."

As they were saying their goodbyes, Ben Stillwater drove past. He waved. Lucy shook her head and kept on walking. Her blond hair was pulled back and she looked all business in her uniform, a gun strapped to her hip.

Eva shook her head at the exchange. "He does whatever he can to rile her."

"Lucy?" Ruby asked, surprised. "I don't know that anything can rile Lucy."

"Ben could rile a sloth." Amelia smiled as she said it. "He enjoys it."

"Yes, I guess he does." Ruby would have said more but she was suddenly aware of the cowboy heading their way, tall and not the type to purposely rile.

"I think this is where I say my goodbyes," Amelia said, a light, parting touch on Ruby's arm. "It's good to have you back in town, Ruby. Let's get that pie at Maggie's next week."

"Thanks. That would be great." Eva and Amelia drifted away, leaving her alone to face Carson.

"Is it something I said?" Carson asked with a heart-stopping grin when he walked up to her.

"I think just the idea of you heading across the street made them all think we had something private to discuss."

"I guess we do."

"Really? Because I think we've said a lot the last few weeks."

He took hold of her arm and headed her up the sidewalk, away from the post office. "I asked the league board to consider giving Derek the scholarship and apprenticeship. I'm going to make a place for him at the ranch working with the horses. He has some real talent, and I'd hate for that to be wasted. He can use the scholarship to study ranch management, maybe equine science."

"Why?"

He turned her to face him. She felt small standing next to him. "I want to help him."

"Is that it?"

He gave her a half grin. "Is there a right answer to these questions? I think even if I'm honest I'm in trouble."

Of their own volition her lips turned and

she laughed a little. "Okay, maybe you have a point."

"You're looking for an argument?"

She shook her head. "No, I'm not. I just don't want him to be in the center of this."

"This?"

She gestured with a hand from herself to him. "I don't want him to be hurt by whatever is going on between us. I learned the hard way that what I think is happening might not be happening. It could be over in the blink of an eye."

"Yes." His voice softened. "Sometimes we're fooled into thinking someone feels what we feel only to find out they don't."

"Not here. Not now. We can't have this discussion on the main street of Little Horn, Texas, with half the town watching." She moved away from him, needing to compose herself, to remember who she was. Without him.

God hadn't brought her home just to have her trip and fall into this well, unable to rescue herself.

"No, not here and not now. Dinner at my house. Next Monday. I'll cook and we can talk."

"About the scholarship?"

He moved a little closer. "About the scholarship, about us, about the past. If we're going to live in the same town, we have to put this to rest. Or…"

She shook her head. "I have to go home. Iva is alone and I can't leave her for long or she's up trying to cook and clean."

"Is there anything I can do?"

"Not unless you know someone looking for a job. I think I'm going to need help taking care of Iva. And she isn't going to like it."

"The only person I know looking for a job is Jenna when she gets back to town."

At that, Ruby got a little off-kilter. "She's coming back. She isn't taking Brandon?"

"No, I'm keeping custody until she can prove to me that she's able to care for him. I'll get a power of attorney for now and she can sign something giving me guardianship."

"That's good. And I think I'll have to look elsewhere for someone." The idea of Jenna in her home with her grandmother? She shook her head, unable to accept the suggestion.

"What did she do?"

"Monday at dinner," she responded. "Not here. Not now. But I can't…" She had started to say she couldn't forgive the things Jenna had said.

But she could. It had been teen drama and it was a dozen years ago. It no longer hurt her. And now, looking at Jenna's life, at her struggles, Ruby didn't have to be angry. Life had a way of changing people.

"Monday," she said as she put space between herself and Carson. Space she realized she didn't really want.

Yes, life had a way of changing people.

Chapter Thirteen

Two days after they talked on the phone Carson led his sister through the old foreman's trailer. They no longer used it. Larry and Gayla held the jobs as head trainers at the ranch. Larry also had the foreman position. The couple were Little Horn natives, though, and had their own small acreage and a house on the edge of town.

"It isn't much," Carson said to his sister. Not as an apology. Jenna had blown through every unprotected cent of her inheritance. She'd had a house that she'd sold. She'd sold her car. She had spent her college money rather than finishing school. She still had a trust fund and a monthly check from the ranch.

"It's a place to live and I can fix it up." She walked from the living room, down the narrow hall to the smaller bedroom and then to the master bedroom at the far end. "Brandon will like this, living close to you."

"Brandon lives *with* me. Don't forget that," he reminded. And when tears welled in her eyes he softened. "For now. Just for now, Jenna."

"I know and I'm glad you're doing this. I'm glad you were here for us. And I'll do better. I want to help at the ranch. I want to be the mom he deserves. All of this time I've known better. I know I wasn't brought up to live the way I've been living. I can't explain it." She closed her eyes and drew in a deep breath, then nodded as she opened her eyes and looked him in the eye. "I can do this. If you don't need me at the ranch, I'll find a job."

"I'm not sure of anyone who is hiring."

"I'm not picky," she said with a smile that didn't flash, wasn't prideful.

Even with everything she'd done, she was his little sister and he was glad to see this side of her again. He remembered the kid she'd once been, full of laughter, smart and willing to try anything. She'd been eleven when they lost their mom and he hadn't realized what it had done to her, to be left without Lila Thorn's soft touch.

She wasn't picky about jobs or where she lived.

"The only person I know who is looking

for help is Ruby Donovan. But I take it there's a problem between the two of you and she doesn't want to hire you."

"No, I don't imagine she does." Jenna looked away from him.

Carson shook his head and stepped away from her. He walked to the wide picture window in the living room. The curtains were dusty rose, the color that had been popular when the trailer had been bought. Now they were mostly just dusty. He shook them out a little and dust particles filled the air.

"What did you do to her?" he asked with his back to his sister.

She joined him at the window, letting her finger trail through dust on the plastic miniblinds. He glanced at his sister, with her long, dark hair and dark eyes. She was taller than average and usually confident. But the confident girl he remembered seemed to have disappeared, swallowed up by someone who'd made too many destructive choices.

"I think she should tell you. But I wasn't good to her, Carson. I was jealous of your relationship. I needed you—"

"You had me." He said it plainly. "You had me and you had everything. She had—"

"She had you." Her tone was insistent.

He pushed his hat back and scratched his

forehead. "Jenna, that's insane. I don't even know what to say to you. But whatever you did or said, I want you to apologize."

"I don't think she'll want to hear it. And why now? Why didn't you have me apologize years ago?"

"Because I didn't know. I had no idea what went on when I was gone. I just know she wasn't here when I got back and that our father paid her to leave."

"That about sums it up. We tore her down. We destroyed her."

"How?" Because up to now he'd thought it was about the money and whatever Jenna had said or done.

"Dad told her if she didn't get her claws out of you, he'd ruin Iva."

That floored him. He'd known his dad could be ruthless, but to threaten Iva Donovan? "You have to be wrong."

"I'm not wrong. I don't know what he planned. Maybe he didn't have a plan. He just knew Ruby was loyal, and if she thought he'd hurt Iva, she'd walk away. It was you or her grandmother. She picked her grandmother."

Anger shook him as he thought about his dad approaching an eighteen-year-old with that type of scheme. Of course she'd left. He would have left. Jenna touched his arm.

"I'm sorry."

He shook himself free from her hand. "That isn't going to change a thing."

"I can't undo what happened, Carson, but I'll talk to her if that's what you want."

"I'm not sure if I want your help."

She walked out the front door and down steps that needed to be repaired. Carson closed the door behind him and followed. The steps were shaky and a few boards had come loose. He'd send a couple of his men over to do the repairs.

"I'm not going to hurt her," Jenna said as she headed for his truck. "I'm going to apologize and make things right. For you."

"Don't do it for me. Do it for yourself. I think you probably have other apologies to make."

"Maybe." She turned back to him. "When we get to the house, can I use your truck?"

"Yeah, I guess you can."

"But first I'd like to see Brandon when he gets home from school. I can tell him how sorry I am and that I'm going to do better. I'm going to be the mom he deserves."

"The mom he deserves is a mom who puts him first. She takes him to church on Sunday. She fixes him dinner every night, tucks him in bed, wakes him up and makes sure he has breakfast before he gets on the bus."

"When you let me, I'll do those things for him."

He opened his truck door. "Let's get back to the house."

Jenna climbed in on the passenger side and she smiled at him, about the most genuine smile he'd seen on her face in a long, long time. He guessed maybe they were getting somewhere. Maybe she would change.

When she proved herself, he'd settle the monthly stipend on her that their dad had left. Money she didn't know about. Didn't need to know about.

Their dad had been a lot of things it seemed, but he'd also been a smart businessman. He'd known his kids and what they could and couldn't handle. When Jenna had left college with her college money, his dad had changed his will.

Carson probably hadn't known himself as well as he'd thought. He hadn't realized how much he would want his nephew to stay in his life. He hadn't realized how much he missed Ruby.

Those were things he was coming to realize. At least where Brandon was concerned, he wasn't too late.

* * *

Someone knocked on the front door. Ruby slid the brush through her hair and gave herself a last critical look in the mirror before going to answer it. She smiled at Iva, who was sitting in her recliner watching an early evening news show.

"I wasn't expecting anyone. Were you?" Ruby asked as she headed for the door.

"No. I guess it isn't Derek's girl. They went to the movies."

Ruby didn't respond because she couldn't. She wanted to believe her brother was at the movies. She needed to believe in him. When she opened the front door, it wasn't Derek's friend Alyssa. It wasn't a friend at all. The woman standing on the other side of the door had changed a lot since high school. She no longer looked like the girl who had everything. She looked a little bit lost and a lot less confident as she stood waiting for a greeting. Ruby didn't quite know what greeting to give.

Jenna Thorn smiled. It was a hesitant gesture, the kind that said she wasn't sure if she'd be welcome. It made sense that she would feel that way. Ruby had a lot of reasons not to welcome Jenna.

There were the old reasons, but those had faded. Teenaged girls could be mean. Life went on. The new and most important reason to dislike Jenna was a five-year-old who had missed his mommy. Brandon. He surprised her by appearing, hurrying up the steps to stand next to his mom.

She opened the door and stepped outside. "Jenna. I didn't expect to see you. Hi, Brandon."

Jenna was thinner than she'd been years ago. Her hair was long. Her eyes were tired. She was two years younger than Ruby but a hard life had aged her. A seed of compassion sprouted. It wasn't forgiveness but maybe it would grow in that direction.

"I came to apologize," Jenna said. She rubbed her hands together in front of her and managed to make eye contact with Ruby. "I'm sorry for what I said."

"Brandon, why don't you run in and watch television with Iva," Ruby offered, and the little boy seemed happy to oblige.

"Good idea," Jenna said, watching her son hightail it inside.

"Wow, this is unexpected." Ruby walked to the end of the porch and took a seat in a rocking chair. Jenna followed her. She didn't sit.

"I know it is. And it's long overdue," Jenna said, leaning against a post. "I wanted to hurt you. I wanted you out of my brother's life."

"I guess you got your way. On both counts."

Jenna finally took a seat. "I'm not proud of who I was or who I've become. I'm going to try and do better. While I've been away I've been going to church and I know this isn't going to be easy. I know what I'm supposed to do and what I need to do. Getting it done, that's the hard part."

"I think you can do it."

"That's nice of you to say," Jenna said. "I know I don't have a lot of fans around here. I know you probably don't think much of me."

"I don't have to. What matters is what you think of yourself."

Truer words she'd never spoken. Ruby had said the same thing to herself as a pep talk all those years ago. She'd said it again just recently.

There was one thing she could do for Jenna. "I forgive you."

Jenna closed her eyes and nodded. A tear trickled down her cheek. "Thank you."

"You're welcome. And now I'm afraid I have to go."

Jenna's eyes were open, her features lit up. "Yes, dinner with Carson. Brandon is spending time with me tonight, but we could stay with Iva if you'd like."

That was taking forgiveness maybe a step

farther than she was comfortable with. She could see that Jenna had made mistakes and needed mercy and a touch of grace. But watching Iva, that was a whole other ballgame.

"I take it that's a no?" Jenna said as she stood to go.

"I don't know if I can go that far, Jenna." She glanced through the open window. She could see Iva clapping as she watched something on TV. Brandon sat next to her, laughing. "She's my grandmother. She means everything to me. Your dad threatened to destroy her. Now, as an adult, I can see that he was bluffing, but that doesn't change anything. I won't let you hurt her."

"I'm not going to defend him, but he thought he was doing the right thing for Carson."

Ruby bristled at the comment that pointed out the differences in their lives. "Yes, I know what he thought he was doing. He was protecting his family by threatening to destroy mine."

Jenna looked away, shaking her head just the tiniest bit. "I don't know what happened to our family. But I'm sorry for what we did to you, to your family. I would like to stay here with Iva. I'm sure she and I would get along, and if she doesn't want me here, I won't stay."

Ruby stood, trying to regain her composure. She hadn't expected this tonight. She hadn't expected to feel anything but anger toward a woman who had taken part in destroying what Ruby held dear. But life changed people. Time had taken the sting out of the words spoken years ago and it had softened the anger she had as a teenager. She guessed she could dredge it all up for old time's sake, but why?

"Come inside."

"She's always been good to me, Ruby. I'm sure she knew what I did to you, but she never held it against me. She used to try to talk to me, to get me to church. I would always brush her off."

"I know. She told me." Ruby moved toward the front door. "She doesn't know what your dad threatened."

"I'm glad you didn't tell her."

"I did it for her, to protect her. I didn't do it for the Thorns."

As they walked through the door, Iva looked up, her eyes twinkling when she saw Jenna. "Well, Jenna Thorn, it has been a long time."

Jenna moved to Ruby's grandmother's side, squatting next to her chair and taking hold of her hand. "It's been too long. But I'm back for good."

"I'm glad you are. And from the look in your eyes, I'm hoping you're back in more way than one. You've come back to yourself, it seems."

"I think so." Jenna lifted the frail, shaking hand she held and placed a kiss on it. "I'd like to stay with you tonight while Ruby goes over for dinner with Carson."

"Suddenly everyone thinks I need a baby-sitter," Iva grumbled. "I don't know what they all think is wrong with me."

"Gran, please…" Ruby stepped forward.

"Oh, don't 'Gran, please' me." Iva's head shook and she wrinkled her nose. "Just go to dinner with that boy. Jenna and Brandon will stay here with me. I don't like to watch *Wheel of Fortune* alone."

"I love to watch *Wheel*," Jenna said as she released Iva's hand and moved to a nearby chair. "You go, Ruby. We'll be just fine."

Ruby looked from her grandmother to Jenna. "I'm not sure."

Iva grunted at that. "I don't know what you have to be sure about. I've made a decision and as far as I know, I'm still of sound mind. You've been worried about me being alone and falling. Now I won't be alone. And I don't think Jenna will push me down."

Jenna and Iva both laughed a little but stopped when Ruby gave them a narrow-eyed look. She shook her head and walked to the door, grabbing her purse on the way. "I'm going."

"Have fun," Iva called out. And then in a quieter voice to Jenna, "I started to think she was no longer able to have fun."

She could have told them that she'd wanted to have fun. She hadn't wanted to lose so much. Or to learn so much about people, about human nature, at such a young age. She knew there were people protected from life. There were children who grew up believing their parents always made the best choices for them. There were children who grew up thinking adults would never harm them.

There were those children.

And then there were the others. Children who were left alone, neglected, abused or just extra baggage that parents didn't want to be bothered with. There were children like Jenna Thorn had been. Children who appeared to have it all but were really very broken on the inside.

Of course she thought of Betsy McKay, Mac McKay's teenage daughter who had disappeared after her father died. As Ruby got in her truck and headed for Carson's, she wondered where the girl had gone to and why no one in the community had taken her in. Maybe Ruby could find her and help her. Maybe she could give the girl a place on the ranch.

She thought of two people who might know the teen's whereabouts. Winston and Gareth McKay. Byron's twin sons. She'd seen them at the gas station a few days earlier and they were growing up. And hopefully not growing into their dad. They'd been respectful. They'd actually been kind. Gareth had even pumped her gas for her. The gesture had taken her by surprise.

Yes, she would talk to them about Betsy.

As she pulled up the drive to the Thorn ranch her thoughts tumbled back to the moment at hand. She'd been able to distract herself for a few minutes, but now reality rushed back. Tonight she and Carson would face their past. She wasn't sure if she was ready.

Trust didn't come easily. He'd hurt her. She'd probably hurt him. How did two people let a dozen years go by and just shrug it off as if it hadn't happened?

She wasn't sure if they did. No matter how good it felt to be together, she wasn't sure if she was ready to just be Carson's girl. She'd become so much more since she'd left. She'd become more than Earl Donovan's daughter. She'd become more than Iva's granddaughter. She'd become Ruby Donovan, a woman people respected.

She didn't know if Carson wanted the woman she'd become in his life or if he wanted the girl he'd once known.

Chapter Fourteen

Carson stirred the spaghetti sauce and then leaned to inhale. Yeah, it was good. It was the one thing he knew he could cook and not mess up. Other than something on the grill. As windy as it was, he had vetoed that idea. He glanced at the clock on the stove. Jenna had called with the news that she would be staying with Iva, and Ruby was on her way and he shouldn't mess it up.

He didn't know how his sister had managed to convince Ruby to let her stay, but he had a moment when he was proud of her for doing this. The past few years had been rough ones and he'd wondered if his sister would make it.

The doorbell chimed. He turned the sauce to simmer and headed for the front door. When he opened it, Ruby snickered a little. That hadn't been the reaction he'd expected.

"I'm not sure my self-esteem can take that," he responded. "People don't usually laugh when I open the door."

"Do you usually wear an apron that says Kiss The Cook?"

He looked down, a little bit embarrassed. Lately, with Brandon in the house, he'd done more cooking. He hadn't given the apron too much thought. It had been a gift from Ben, who had thought it was funny. Carson didn't agree with his friend's humor, but he used the apron anyway.

"I guess I hadn't paid much attention." He yanked the thing over his head.

She laughed, this time a real laugh, the kind that had her wiping tears from under her eyes. He felt his mouth tilt at the corners, but he pushed the gesture away.

"Something smells good," she said as he led her through the house to the kitchen.

"Spaghetti. Is that okay?"

"Of course it is. Do you get your sauce from a jar?"

"Absolutely not." He headed for the stove. "Homemade sauce. It's the only thing I can cook other than what I throw on the grill."

"Jenna is with my grandmother," she said as she took a seat at the island. "I didn't expect to see her."

"No, I guess I should have warned you."

She shrugged. "Probably better that you didn't. Sometimes a surprise attack is best. I wasn't able to prepare myself to be angry."

He turned from the stove, spoon in hand. She smiled again, her eyes crinkling at the corners.

"You do make a cute chef."

"Thank you," he said. "I think."

"It was a compliment," she said, her voice trailing off to a softness that had him moving toward her.

"We should eat before we talk."

She nodded. "Yes, we should. But I don't know if I can wait. I don't know how to do this."

"I know that my dad threatened Iva." He couldn't soften the words. It still made him angry.

"Jenna told you?"

"Yeah. The only thing she wouldn't tell me is what she did."

She got up and helped herself to a glass of tea from the pitcher on the counter. She stood in the corner of the kitchen, leaning against the cabinet, the glass between her hands. He wanted to move closer. He knew better.

This wasn't the girl he'd known all those

years ago. She was a woman who knew herself, knew what she wanted.

"It was silly girl drama," she said from her place in the corner of his kitchen. "It hurt, but it wasn't the end of the world. Just the average gossip about the Donovans and how we bought our clothes secondhand. She said one thing that mattered. She said you had found someone at college who was better for you than I would ever be. Here I was thinking you'd come home over the summer and we'd make plans for the future. I know I was just eighteen, but I loved you, Carson. I wanted to spend my life with you. It broke my heart to think that I could be so easily replaced."

"You were never replaced, Ruby. There was no one but you. Jenna did that because she was jealous of you. She needed more attention. She was lonely and missing our mom and she took that out on you."

Her eyes glittered with unshed tears and when he started to move toward her she held up a hand, stopping him. "I would have left anyway."

The words froze him. "The money? Was it really that important? You had scholarships."

She brushed a hand across her eyes and shook her head. "I didn't take the stupid check, Carson. I mean I took it and then I ripped it up.

Your dad knew that. He would have known because it never came out of his account."

The circle of deception amazed him. His dad and his sister had done everything in their power to hurt her.

"Carson, he threatened Iva. I couldn't let him hurt her. Now, as an adult, I realize he couldn't have done anything to my grandmother. If he'd tried, people would have rallied around her. But I didn't know. I just knew that if I left, she'd be safe. My brother would be safe. Now I'm back and they're the farthest thing from safe. Every single day I worry that something will happen and that Derek will be arrested, charged with these thefts."

"If he's innocent, that won't happen."

"If?"

He knew he'd messed up by the way her eyes narrowed and the word came out like a hiss.

"He isn't going to be arrested for crimes he hasn't committed." And still it sounded wrong.

The spaghetti sauce was bubbling and he could feel this dinner heading south. He reached to turn off the burner and then he focused on the woman standing in his kitchen, her back straight.

"This is why we won't work, Carson. Because we're always going to be the couple that doesn't fit. My life and yours, we're worlds apart. Your sister comes home from living a life that included neglecting her child and she's immediately sheltered, protected and people will forgive her. Because she's a Thorn.

"Derek is always going to be the suspect in every crime because when he was eighteen he stole something. I'm not going to call it a mistake. It was a crime that he committed and it was wrong. But he should be allowed to change just the same as Jenna is allowed to change."

"I agree."

"But…"

He didn't know what to say. He did know enough about women to know that he probably couldn't say the right thing at this point.

"Derek and Jenna have both made mistakes. They both deserve forgiveness." He didn't mean for the hopeful tone to sneak in to the words, almost as if he was asking her to approve of what he'd just said.

"Yes, they do. I'm done with this town, Carson. I'm done living here where everyone points fingers at the Donovans. I'm the offspring of a man who sold off half his family land in order to fund his rodeo career. I'm the woman who took your daddy's money to walk away from you. I'm the sister of Derek Donovan, the ex-con."

"You're a woman who is strong and takes care of her family."

The right words. Her features softened.

"Is it enough, Carson? Is it ever going to be enough? Or should we sell off and leave Little Horn? Derek could have a fresh start somewhere else. We could find a town where he isn't always the suspect."

"Maybe that isn't what he wants?" He dished her up a plate of spaghetti as he talked. "Try letting people make their own choices, Ruby. I would have chosen you."

She took the plate with hands that trembled. "You might have. Or you might have given in to pressure. If I hadn't left, I think your dad would have found other ways to force us apart."

"He might have," he said, fixing his own plate. "But that's all in the past."

"Right, but the present isn't exactly smooth sailing."

He led her to the dining room. He'd bought flowers, lit candles and managed to make the place appear halfway romantic. He doubted she would notice. She took a seat at one end of the table, leaving him the head of the table. He sat, reaching for her hand to pray.

The gesture must have surprised her. She looked up, her lips slightly parted.

"I'm going to pray, Ruby. And I'm going

to remind you that life doesn't guarantee us smooth sailing."

"I know. I really do know that. I keep thinking that God has some greater plan for all of this. For the doubts, for Derek, for our community. How do we get through this if we lose sight of what is important, our faith and our community, and start to tear each other apart with suspicion and accusation?"

"I think the community has to be reminded of that." He lifted the hand he held and kissed it. And then he prayed.

They were taking their first bites when his cell phone rang. It was Lucy. He shook his head, not wanting to answer but knowing he had to.

"This can't be good."

"Who is it?" Ruby asked as he lifted the phone to his ear.

"Lucy," he said.

She went a little pale and pushed away her plate. He listened as Lucy filled him in on what was going on, and then he ended the call and set his phone on the table.

"This isn't good, is it?" Ruby asked.

"The McKay place got hit again. This is the second time this month."

"Great."

"Let's take a drive over there," Carson suggested. "After we eat."

"As if I can eat another bite."

Carson had to agree. "I guess you aren't going to comment on the flowers and the candlelight?"

She smiled at that, reaching to touch a rose in the bouquet at the center of the table. "They are beautiful. You had Bobbi Ann do this, didn't you?"

"A guy who wears a Kiss The Cook apron has a few skills other than cooking."

She stood, picked up his plate and stacked it on hers. "I think I should leave the room while I can."

"You're hard on a man's self-esteem."

"Maybe I'm here to keep you from thinking too highly of yourself," she teased.

He took the plates from her hands and set them in the sink. And then, before she could think twice, because he didn't want her to think, he pulled her close. Her lips parted and he took advantage, covering her mouth with his. She felt good in his arms. She felt right.

She was wrong. The present wasn't such a terrible place to be.

But it was a complicated place. He brushed his lips over hers, kissed her slow and steady, holding her close. And then he eased away from her.

"We should go," she reminded in a soft voice that made him want to never leave. He kept his hands on her waist, wanting to pull her to him again.

"We should definitely go," he admitted. "But we're not finished, Ruby."

She didn't agree. Instead, she found her purse and headed for the front door. He knew the reason for her hurry. She was afraid that Derek would be accused. Byron McKay had it out for the younger man. He'd always had it out for the Donovans. It had something to do with a girl in high school. That's what Carson's dad had once told him. Byron McKay and Earl Donovan had both wanted the same girl. Earl had gotten her.

That girl had been Derek and Ruby's mom. He would have thought it would make Byron a little kinder to them. Maybe they reminded him too much of what he'd lost.

He could understand how he'd feel. He knew how it had felt to lose Ruby. He knew how he felt when she talked about leaving town.

Blue lights flashed through the night sky. Ruby clasped her hands in her lap as Carson drove his truck through the gate and up the driveway of the McKay ranch. The place was huge. Sprawling. The house was enormous. The acreage was vast. The outbuildings were larger than some department stores.

How did someone with this much even know that he'd lost something? Byron could lose his family on this place for days and not realize he was alone.

"My mom dated him, you know," she spoke into the silent cab of the truck.

"Yeah, my dad told me."

"She said it was better to be church-mouse poor with a man who loved her than to live like royalty with a man who would have made her miserable."

"Wise woman," he said as he pulled to a stop behind a state trooper's car.

"Yes, she was." Ruby got out of the truck and the two of them walked up to the big barn.

They couldn't miss Byron. He stood in front of Lucy waving his hands as he roared about being hit twice and how she should do her job. Ruby figured that kind of response wouldn't make Lucy want to keep his place safe from thieves.

"So would it be safe to assume that the thief isn't too fond of Byron McKay," she whispered to Carson.

He laughed at that. "I'd say that makes about half the county suspects."

Byron spotted them. "Where's that brother of yours?"

Lucy put a hand on his arm. "Byron, we're here to investigate, and it won't help anyone if you start pointing fingers."

"I've lost thousands of dollars in machinery and tack. I'm not going to let you mess up this investigation because you don't want to hurt anyone's feelings." He took a few steps and was face-to-face with Ruby.

She tried to stand a little taller and ignored Carson next to her, because this wasn't his fight. "Byron, my brother is out on a date."

"And you think he couldn't talk that little girl into covering for him?" Byron slammed the words out, his anger fueling his voice to a decibel Ruby wouldn't have believed possible.

She purposefully kept her voice soft, making him lean in to listen. "I'm sure she does like him, but just because they are dating doesn't mean she'd stoop to criminal activity to protect him. I'm not sure how insulting everyone in the county is going to catch a thief. Byron, the only thing you're doing is destroying a community that has always stayed together. How will Little Horn survive if everyone starts accusing and back-biting?"

"That isn't really my concern, little girl." He spat the words.

Ruby wiped her cheek and looked him in the eye. "I'm not your little girl."

"No, you aren't."

Lucy stepped between them. "Ruby, have you seen Derek this evening?"

At that Ruby groaned. "So you are accusing him?"

Lucy expression softened. "No, but I have to ask. He was seen walking down the highway about two hours ago."

"He's with Alyssa Meadows. She picked him up at five this afternoon. I don't know where they went after that."

"I need to talk to him," Lucy said, her gaze darting from Ruby to Carson. "It's just procedure."

"Right. I understand." Ruby let out a sigh. She hated this. She hated that her brother was a suspect. She hated the tiny seed of doubt that had been planted in her own mind. Because she'd seen him leave with Alyssa. They'd been on their way to her parents' place for dinner and then to the movies.

"I'll have him come in tomorrow." Lucy turned back to her officer and the state officer that were on scene. "Let's see what we can find. Remember to look for tire tracks, and we'll see if we can't put the same vehicle at all of our robberies."

Ruby backed away from the scene. She backed away from Carson, who had stopped to talk to one of the officers. Tom Horton, a local rancher and not someone Ruby had ever known well, stepped up to talk to the group. He was one of the men involved in the newly formed league investigation committee.

Out of nowhere the McKay twins appeared. They stood back a little behind their dad. As Ruby waited for Carson they shot her twin looks of sympathy. She smiled at the boys, sorry for them because they had to listen to their dad run down everyone in their community. When he started in on Betsy McKay, cousin to the boys, Gareth and Winston stepped forward. She couldn't hear them but she knew they were defending the girl, who now seemed to be on the list of suspects.

Ruby thought that if the suspects included everyone in the county who had a problem with Byron McKay, the list would be long and complicated.

"Ready to go?" Carson appeared at her side. For a moment she was glad to have him there. He stood at her side, sheltering her, making her feel less alone in this chaotic scene.

Until Tom Horton spoke to Lucy, just a short

distance away, telling her that Carson agreed that she should bring Derek Donovan in for questioning.

"I'm walking home." She turned to leave.

Carson caught her by the arm. "Do not walk away from me."

"Do not tell me what to do. I'm walking." She yanked her arm free. She had to keep walking because tears were streaming down her cheeks and she didn't want him to see her cry.

"Ruby, he has to answer the questions or no one will ever believe he's innocent." Carson caught up with her. He walked next to her, still talking. "He was seen walking down the road. That makes him a suspect."

She held a hand up. "I can't talk about this right now. I just want to leave. I want to leave this ranch and this town."

"Now you're being—"

"Emotional, yes, I know. I had forgotten how it felt to be here, to be a Donovan. For the past eight years I've been an employee for the state of Oklahoma, in a community where people respected me and respected my position."

"People respect you here."

She shook her head. "I'm going home, Carson."

"Let me drive you." He put a hand on hers

and led her to the truck. "At least let me take you home."

She closed her eyes briefly and nodded. "I'm so tired of this. I'm tired of fighting for..."

"For us?"

"I don't know. I'm tired of fighting everything. I'm fighting to save a ranch. Fighting to save my grandmother and my brother. I'm just tired, Carson. I'm really tired. And I don't have enough energy for anything else."

He brushed a hand down her cheek, smudging the tears with his thumb. "You're beautiful."

She opened the truck door and climbed in, the weariness making her ache deep down, all the way to her heart. She'd counted on him. Maybe that was wrong, but she'd wanted him to defend Derek. She'd wanted him to be more, do more.

And maybe that wasn't fair, but it was the truth. She needed him. At her side.

But she couldn't have him. Not right now. Not with the entire town being pulled apart. Not now, when she wondered if they would even be able to keep this ranch and stay in Little Horn.

"I might need to sell the ranch to pay for lawyers," she admitted. "If that happens, will you buy it?"

"Of course I will. And you can stay in the house. Iva should be able to stay in her home."

Yes, Iva should. She wanted this all to go away. She didn't want to feel like a coward, always running from the court of public speculation.

She wanted to stay in this town with this man. And she wanted life to be easy.

That wouldn't happen. The grown-up side of her knew that life was never easy and that faith grew from tribulation. But part of her wanted to stomp her feet and yell, "Enough!"

Chapter Fifteen

"You can leave." Ruby hadn't meant to speak so harshly to Jenna. After all, this time it wasn't her fault. "I'm sorry. I'm home and thank you for staying with Gran."

"Gran can thank Jenna herself," Iva said, stepping into the living room with her walker. "The girl helped me get cleaned up. We put clean sheets on my bed. She's a keeper, Ruby."

Ruby briefly closed her eyes and nodded. When she looked up, Jenna and Gran were both watching her. "What?"

"Are you okay?" Jenna asked, handing her a glass of water. "He didn't poison you with his cooking, did he? He never could cook more than meat on the grill."

"I'm just tired. There was another incident tonight. The McKay place again."

"Again?" Iva headed for her chair, easing

down with jerking movements that unsettled Ruby and had Jenna hurrying to the older woman's side.

"Yes, again. Gran, we need to talk." Ruby stood in the center of the tiny living room where she'd spent the best years of her life. The best. Broke as they'd been, even with those who thought they were a little bit too good for the Donovans, it had been good here.

"That's my cue to go." Jenna scooped up the sleeping Brandon. "For what it's worth, he loves you."

Ruby nodded and she let it go. She didn't need to hear that he loved her. She couldn't take hearing those words. The door clicked quietly behind Jenna's departure.

And then it opened again and Derek stepped inside, giving her a cautious look as he kicked off his boots.

"What's up at the McKay place? Another burglary?"

"Ruby is about to tell us. Have a seat, Derek." Gran nodded toward the sofa. "Sit down, Ruby, before you fall down."

"I'm afraid if I sit, I won't get back up."

Iva laughed a little. "Welcome to my world. Now sit down, you're making me tired looking at you."

Ruby sat down and she locked gazes with her brother. "Where were you tonight?"

"With Alyssa's family."

She'd known that plan. "You were seen walking down the highway. In front of the McKays'."

"Great, now you're going to paint me as a suspect. I didn't go anywhere near that ranch. Alyssa picked me up and we headed to her place."

"Then why is someone saying they saw you?"

"I don't know why, but I'll find out. It wasn't me."

"How'd you buy the necklace?" The second the words left her mouth she wanted them back. She wanted to undo the hurt look on her brother's face.

"I bought it with money. I'm going to bed. And as soon as I can, I'm moving."

"You're going to have to talk to Lucy."

"I'm not talking to anyone." With that he walked out the door, and a few minutes later they heard his truck fire up and head down the drive.

"You could have handled that better." Iva's voice shook as she spoke. "I know it's hard, trying to be the head of this family, Ruby. But you have to trust. You have to stick together. You've only got each other."

Ruby couldn't look at her grandmother. "We have you."

"Yes, you have me. But you won't always have me. I've done my best, and now it's up to you."

"I want to sell the ranch. Carson says he'll buy it."

"And where would we go?"

She shrugged and finally looked at her grandmother. "Back to Oklahoma. I can get my job back. We can live in my little house."

"You leased it out for a year."

"We can live somewhere else until the lease is up."

Iva pushed herself to her feet, using the handles of the walker. "I'm not moving. I'm not selling this ranch. And we are not running from this. Stay and fight. Try trusting God to do something with this situation."

"I'm trying," Ruby insisted.

Iva stopped her slow progress from the room. "Lip service and real action are two different things, Ruby Jo Donovan. God is going to do something in this situation. He's going to use it to teach some lessons, to solve some problems and whatever else He sees fit to do with it. You running from it won't help matters at all."

"I want to protect my brother."

"Then believe he's innocent."

She nodded, but her grandmother was already heading down the hall to her room. Ruby got up and went after her.

"Gran, I love you." She caught up with Iva as she walked through the door of her bedroom.

"If you love me, help me get into that bed. And then go spend some time with God, because that's the only way you're going to find any peace in this situation. And tomorrow, I'm assuming you'll have to make peace with Carson."

"I think that ship has sailed. He wants Lucy to question Derek."

"There's probably a reason."

"Maybe there is, but I'd like for him to defend my brother and tell people he believes he's innocent."

Iva patted her cheek with a hand that shook in a heartbreaking way. "Oh, Ruby, you do want it all."

Ruby wrapped her arms around her grandmother and held her. "I'm so glad we have you. Thank you."

"No, thank you. For coming home. I've missed having you here. And I'm going to be sadly disappointed to leave this earth without seeing you married and happy. I never thought

I'd see the day that Derek would be the one set-tling down. Not that I'm not happy for him."

"You aren't leaving this earth anytime soon, so don't talk like that."

Iva's face lit up as she sat down on her bed. "That's good to hear. That gives you time to marry and make sure I have great-grandchil-dren."

"Now you've gone too far." She helped her grandmother get settled, and then she kissed her brow and smoothed her gray hair. "I love you," she said again.

"Oh, honey, I love you, too."

She walked to the front door and looked out. Somewhere in the distance she heard a truck engine. She stepped out, wondering if it was Derek's truck. He needed to come home. If he was out there alone it made him a suspect all over again. The last thing he needed to do was give people another reason to suspect him.

The advice her grandmother had given seemed to take precedence over her fears. She needed to pray and trust that God had this sit-uation firmly under control. Her worries and fears weren't going to change a thing. But her faith might.

For the first time in a lot of years, the Thorns went to church as a family. Carson and Brandon had picked up Jenna at the trailer she'd been working on all weekend. The three of them pulled into the parking lot of Little Horn Community Christian Church a few minutes later.

"There's Ruby!" Brandon let out a whoop of excitement. "And Derek."

"Yes, there they are." Carson watched as they got out of their car, and then Derek moved to help Iva out of the front passenger seat.

"Can I get out?" Brandon already had his seat belt off and the door pushed open.

"To the sidewalk and be careful not to plow Iva down," Jenna warned.

They watched as her son hurried to greet the Donovans. It took everything in Carson not to go after the boy. Next to him, Jenna cleared her throat.

"I'm not sure what you did to Ruby, but after all the work I went to, smoothing the way for you, I'm disappointed."

"Disappointed?" He took his keys out of the ignition. "Let's go to church."

"Yeah," she said when they met on the sidewalk. She smiled up at him, almost her old self. He hoped she didn't lose that part of herself again. "I thought you would make things right and instead she came home looking like someone who had completely given up."

"She…" He shook his head. "I'm not having this conversation."

"Fine, go ahead and be stubborn. All of those years ago you should have gone after her. You should have found out the truth. Instead, you shrugged it off and said if she wanted to go, she should go."

"You can't force someone to stay in your life."

"No, you can't, you stubborn fool. But sometimes people don't want to go. Sometimes they leave because they think it's the only option. She didn't feel as if she had options."

"Is that how you felt?" he asked, curious.

"Maybe. I don't know. I needed time to think and to realize what's important." She cleared her throat. "I joined a support group. I'm going to keep getting help."

"I would have—"

"Carson." She smiled and stopped him. "I'm an alcoholic. You couldn't have helped."

The news shouldn't have shocked him, but it did. He didn't know what to say. But Brandon was heading their way and he couldn't say anything.

"It's okay." Jenna filled the void and then turned to hug her son.

He hugged his mom tight and then hugged Carson.

"I'm going to my class," Brandon called out as he hurried away again.

"Be good," Jenna called out after him. He was already heading for the door to the classrooms.

They found a seat at the front of the church. Carson remembered this pew with his mom and his sister. Their dad had never come. He hadn't been a man to sit through a sermon, he'd said, when he knew God, and God knew he had a ranch to run. Carson tried to pinpoint when he'd become James Thorn. Maybe when he came home to find Ruby gone.

The sermon that day started out about having giving hearts. But then Pastor Mathers, not much older than Carson, stopped midsentence. He looked out at his congregation and shook his head.

"Today I see neighbor divided against neighbor. I see you all whispering, pointing. Let's just call it what it is, gossip. Bearing false witness. I see the worst of human nature right here in our congregation. And I wonder when it will stop. Who will be the godly leaders to put a stop to this bitterness that could easily divide this town? Could even divide this church? I see you all here each Sunday, and I know that most of you have been in church your entire lives. So today I'm going to ask you to behave like people who have been in church your entire lives."

Someone shouted an "Amen."

Pastor Mathers continued. "There are those of you who think this thief is the worst among you. I'll remind you of a man who died on a cross, who was told by our Savior, 'Today you will be with me in paradise.' Forgiven. I would like to believe we have compassion and forgiveness. It is wrong to steal. But the rest of this, the anger and pointing fingers, how is that any better? In the middle of all of this chaos, I see something else that inspires. Someone is giving to neighbors in need. Someone, we don't know who, is looking with open eyes and seeing that there are those among us who could use help. And I wonder why haven't we all looked to see who we could help? I'm going to end our sermon with this. I don't know how long this will go on, but we have a choice. We can be strong together. Or we can let our community fall apart. You all have to make the decision."

Byron McKay got up and walked out.

Carson joined the others in applauding their pastor and his bravery. It had had to be said. He'd needed to hear it. Now if they could just remember it until the thief or thieves were caught.

After they were dismissed, he stood and

glanced around the church for Ruby. She was at the back, seated next to her grandmother and Derek. They made eye contact but she quickly looked away.

He started toward her but Tom Horton stepped in his way, blocking not only his view but his path to Ruby.

"Carson, we need to talk about Friday night."

"What about it, Tom?" He glanced past the other man and saw Ruby heading for the door. Derek walked next to their grandmother, shielding her.

"We were out patrolling and we saw Derek Donovan driving around the back roads."

"Not a crime that I'm aware of." Carson tried to step around the other man. "I hate to end this conversation this way, but I need to go."

Tom glanced back over his shoulder and then he pinned Carson with a steel-gray look. "I realize you and Ruby have had a relationship over the years. That doesn't mean we can ignore Derek. He was slowing down, looking at fences. They saw him at the Hansen place, out of his truck and walking down fence rows."

"And you didn't call the police? Lucy is the one who needs to hear this, not me."

"I'm going to tell Lucy tomorrow morning. But you have to admit, the local law hasn't done much to solve this crime."

"Tom, they're working on it. The last thing we need to do is start running down our law enforcement." He started to remind the other man of the sermon they'd just listened to, but Lynette Fields appeared, looking flustered. And Lynette never looked flustered.

"We're going to have to call a meeting this next week."

"Why is that?" Carson asked.

Lynette gave Tom Horton a narrow-eyed look. "Because some members of our committee want to see Derek Donovan arrested without sufficient evidence. Also, Lucy has the list of items stolen and the details, so we can take a look and see if anyone can think of something we've missed that might point to the thief." She paused and let out a sigh.

"And?" Carson prompted.

"Byron said he wants the recipients of any gifts investigated. That means the Bunkers and everyone else. Millicent Anders had a load of hay show up, then there were the saddles at Ruby's and even that cowhand who found some nice boots and gloves at his place."

"This is crazy," Carson said. "I'm sorry, but I don't know if I can call a meeting for more neighbor-against-neighbor bullying."

"It isn't bullying," Tom said. "It's an investigation. We have to look at everyone."

Carson shook his head. "Call your meeting. I'll be there. But I want it known that I don't approve, and if this continues, I'm resigning."

He headed out the front door, catching up with Ruby and her family as they were getting into their car. "Ruby, as members of the league, you all need to know that there is a meeting tomorrow. I want you to be there."

Ruby shook her head. "I'm not going to your meetings. I'm not the member and Gran has resigned from the board."

"They're calling into question everyone who has received an anonymous gift," he told her. "I'm under the impression that no one really listened to the sermon."

"Well, we'd be a far sight better off if they had," Iva Donovan said as she let Derek help her into the car. "I'll be at that meeting, Carson. And I'll see if I can't get my stubborn grand-daughter to show up, too."

"I have lessons tomorrow afternoon," Ruby informed them with a little smile. "I'm sorry, I won't be there."

Carson ran a hand over the top of his head and tried to think of something to get her to listen. He'd rather have her mad and arguing than this passive person who wouldn't fight.

She got behind the wheel of the car, started it up and backed out of the parking space. Carson watched her go and then he turned. Lucy Benson stood behind him. Her gaze followed the departing sedan and then shifted to him.

"We're going to bring him in for questioning," she said. At his look she shrugged. "I don't really have a choice. He was at the Meadowses' place last night, but then he was seen by himself walking along fences. I'm going to have to find out why."

"I know you are."

"I don't want to cause problems between you and Ruby. It seemed like the two of you were working things out."

"Yeah, we were." He pulled his keys out of his pocket. "I have to get home."

Jenna and Brandon were heading his way. They were talking; Brandon's hand was in his mom's. Everything else seemed to be falling apart. At least this was going in the direction that it needed to go. His family seemed stronger than it had been in years.

But just as he thought maybe he had a chance with Ruby, things looked like they were going south.

Chapter Sixteen

Ruby had no intention of going to the meeting on Monday. But she guessed she wouldn't be having a riding class, either. None of her students had showed up. Derek had driven Iva to the meeting, taking the sedan. Ruby drove her old farm truck to Little Horn.

Town was busy, maybe because it was a pretty day, or maybe because it was the last week of the month. The grocery store parking lot was packed for a Monday. Ruby parked in front of Maggie's and glanced inside. Nearly every table was full. At four in the afternoon. She continued down the street, saying hi to neighbors she met. At least those who would speak to her.

She happened to glance down the street in the direction of the police station and saw her brother walk through the door with Lucy

Benson. Ruby's feet froze as she watched. She hadn't been in town last time. Iva had handled it all. Ruby had come home on weekends to give their grandmother emotional support.

This time they were together. But Iva didn't need this. They wouldn't survive it. She glanced at the store building. Someone had put a flea market in the old Five-And-Dime. She didn't want to keep walking. She didn't want to meet any more neighbors and pretend everything was okay. To avoid skeptical eye contact and awkward greetings, she stepped into the Little Horn Flea Market.

The owner, a man she didn't recognize, greeted her with a smile. "Anything I can help you find?"

"No, I'm just looking." Truth be told she was avoiding. But this stranger didn't need to know that.

"You new to town?" he asked.

She shook her head. "No, but I've been gone awhile."

He went back to work dusting figurines on a shelf. Ruby stopped at a case of jewelry. She'd never been one to wear jewelry. An occasional bracelet, sometimes a necklace, but that was it. But she did like to look. She always thought she'd wear turquoise if she wore anything.

Her gaze settled on a row of belt buckles.

She scanned the engravings, stopping at the last one. She turned to the owner of the shop.

"This buckle. The championship buckle. Where did you get that?"

He climbed down off his ladder, a little out of breath, and walked back behind the counter. She pointed through the glass and he nodded, smiling. "That's a real beaut, isn't it?"

"Yes, but where did you get it?"

"Kid came in a week or so ago and asked if I bought gold or silver. I do from time to time, but this is worth more than the silver. It's a collector's item. Did you know there are kids who collect anything they can of Earl Donovan's?"

"Why?" Her heart beat a little unsteadily, making her feel shaky.

"He was a real champion. I know it was fifteen years ago, give or take, but he made an impression. The kid who sold me this was his son. I asked why he'd want to get rid of something so important and he said it was time to let go of the past."

"Yes, it is." She swiped at a tear trickling down her cheek. "What did he get for it?"

"A necklace. A real nice sapphire piece. He has a girlfriend. Said she's more important to him than a keepsake."

Ruby nodded and walked away. She'd started to doubt her brother. Now she had to go tell

Lucy what she'd found. As she headed toward the police station, Amelia Klondike caught up with her.

"Ruby, are you okay?"

Ruby slowed her pace to let the other woman get next to her. "Yes, I'm fine. I just found out something. I need to talk to Lucy."

"What's going on?"

"Byron McKay mentioned a necklace Derek's girlfriend was wearing. I know where he got it."

Amelia linked arms with her. "That's great. Let me go with you. And maybe afterward you can come down to the house for some iced tea. I think you could use a break."

"I could, but I'm not sure I'll have time, I…" What did she have to do? "That would be nice."

She would enjoy sitting on the porch of Amelia's pretty Victorian home, drinking sweet tea and pretending all was right in the world.

Instead, she entered the police station, where the officer sitting behind the desk gave her a serious look and then nodded in the direction of Lucy's office. "She's back there."

"I'll wait here for you," Amelia said. She took a seat in one of the old wood chairs lined up against the wall.

Ruby knocked on the door to Lucy's office.

"Come in," Lucy called out.

She entered the room expecting her brother to be handcuffed or at least upset. Instead, he smiled up at her as she walked in. And for whatever reason, that upset her. If she was worried, he should be worried.

"Ruby, have a seat. Are you okay?" Lucy pointed to a nearby chair.

"I'm good. I just came from the flea market." Derek cleared his throat. "Uh-oh."

"You traded Dad's belt buckle for the necklace. The one Byron is insinuating that you stole. Or bought with money from stolen merchandise." She rubbed a hand down her face. "Why didn't you tell the truth? You wouldn't be here if you'd told the truth."

"Ruby, Derek and I have been talking. I know people want to point fingers, but he found some evidence last night that we've missed."

"That's why I was out walking the fence lines the other night, Ruby." He picked up a piece of a taillight. "I'm not guilty and the last thing I want is for you to believe that. Or for this to cause problems between you and Carson. I went looking, thinking I might be able to find something that got overlooked."

Lucy took the red plastic from him and put it in a bag. "I'm not sure how my guys overlooked this. And I know that people like Byron will continue to point fingers, but this will help us maybe get a better lead on the truck or the trailer."

"Derek is no longer a suspect?"

Lucy looked from Ruby to her brother and inclined her head. "He's free to go. Stay away from the McKays and the McKay ranch."

Derek stood but his gaze landed on Ruby. "Why aren't you at the ranch with your students?"

"None of them showed." But she didn't want to talk about that. When Derek tried, she raised her hand. "It isn't as if I'm making a lot off the riding lessons. I went online last night and applied for some state jobs."

"In this state, right?" Derek asked as they walked out. Amelia was still waiting and she stood when she saw them.

"Not all of them. Sorry, Derek. I will have to go where the job is. And now I'm going to Amelia's for a glass of iced tea. You can get Gran home from the meeting, right?"

"Yeah, I'll get her home from the meeting. And I'm going to have a talk with Carson Thorn," he mumbled as he walked off.

"Please don't," she called out after him.

The last thing she needed was her brother inserting himself into her relationship with Carson.

* * *

Carson watched out the window of the board room of the league building. Derek came out of the police station first, and he didn't look like a man in trouble. Ruby came out next, walking next to Amelia Klondike. The two headed on foot in the direction of Amelia's big house.

Tom Horton cleared his throat. "We could get back to the meeting if you're done window shopping?"

"There's not much more to say. Lucy left the list. And I don't see that any of us want to start watching the people who have been given gifts as if they're criminals. They're good people who've fallen on hard times, and someone met a need for them. That doesn't make them suspect. Lucy says the same."

"What about that Donovan kid?" one of the members asked.

Iva Donovan thumped her hand on the table. "'That Donovan kid' is my grandson. And he isn't the thief. You all are going to miss the real culprits focusing on everyone else. This is why we have law enforcement, to keep citizens from making a mess of things."

"I have to agree with Iva," Lynette Fields spoke up. She glanced at her watch. "I have to run. Is there a reason Ben Stillwater didn't show up to this meeting?"

Carson shook his head. "Not that I know of. I'll give him a call."

"They haven't had any things taken, have they?" Byron McKay spoke up, and he'd been pretty quiet for the most part.

"No, Byron. So I think we ought to go get Ben right now and arrest him." With that, Carson got up and walked out.

His phone rang as he was heading for his truck. He thought about not answering. He'd like to catch up with Ruby and talk things out. Instead, he glanced at the caller ID and saw that it was Ben.

"Where are you?"

Ben laughed, but it was shaky and not exactly filled with humor. "Well, I'm at home and I've got a problem."

"You're the thief. We figured as much."

There was a long pause that took Carson by surprise. He counted on Ben for one thing, his ability to never take anything too seriously.

"Ben?"

"Carson, are you on your way to your place?"

"Yeah, why?"

"Care if I come over? I could use a level head about now and I'm pretty sure mine doesn't count."

"You driving or riding?"

"Riding. I need fresh air and a few minutes to think."

Carson opened the door to his truck. "Care to tell me what's going on?"

"Might as well." There was another long pause. "Carson, someone left a baby on my doorstep. Knocked and just left it there."

"A baby…" Carson thought about it for a second. "A baby kitten. Or a puppy."

No one in their right mind would leave a human baby with Ben Stillwater. He could handle a puppy, a kitten, even a calf or a foal. But a human being?

"A baby, Carson. A living, breathing, human being. Mamie says it looks like a Stillwater."

Mamie Stillwater, Ben's grandmother, ought to know a thing or two about babies, especially ones that looked like Stillwaters. "Okay, a baby. But where did it come from and have you called Lucy?"

"I don't know where it came from and no, I haven't called Lucy. She isn't a huge fan of mine and she's not going to be impressed by a baby with a note that says, 'Your baby, your turn.'"

Carson whistled. "Buddy, your chickens have come home to—"

"Not in the mood, Carson. Just be at your place when I get there."

"I'll be waiting. Text me a picture of the little Ben."

"How do you know it isn't a little Grady?"

He counted back. It had been a few months since any of them had seen Grady, who was now stationed in Afghanistan. "I guess it could be."

"Yeah, it could."

"If it's yours, do you have any idea who it might belong to?" Carson started his truck and backed out of the parking space.

"Yeah, I have ideas. I'll see you at your place."

Carson tossed his phone on the seat and headed home. He drove past the Donovan place, but he didn't stop. Later. He'd talk to Ruby later. He'd ask her about the Realtor he'd seen at their house. He'd tell her they could learn to work things out instead of walking away every time things got a little difficult.

He pulled up to his place and parked out front instead of in the garage. He figured he had about fifteen minutes before Ben showed up. He'd grab a cup of coffee, eat a piece of the pie Bobbi Ann left the night before and then head out to the barn. Because the stable was where he and Ben always had their heart-to-heart man talks. That's what Mamie Stillwater called them. And she laughed because she'd always said they weren't men until they had more than two whiskers on their chins.

Ben didn't show up in fifteen minutes. Or in thirty. Carson groomed his gelding. He cleaned a couple of stalls. He found one of the hands that was still working and told him to go home.

And then he headed for the house. As he headed up the steps to the front door, Lucy pulled up. He waited on the porch for her.

From the serious frown on her face, this wasn't a social call. Great, now he was a suspect? He walked down off the steps and met her in the yard.

"Lucy, what's up?"

"Carson, it's about Ben."

"Yeah, I know about the baby. I told him to call you."

"It isn't about the baby. Carson, Ben is in the Little Horn hospital, unconscious. He was riding, probably too—" She broke off and he thought he saw a glimmer of tears in her eyes. She took in a deep breath. "He's unconscious. One of his hands found him on the ground, the horse a short distance away."

She glanced away, the breeze blowing her hair around her face. "It doesn't look good. We're going to try to reach Grady."

"He's going to be fine, Lucy."

She put a hand on his arm. "He's always fine, isn't he?"

"Yeah, he is. Did he say anything? Or was he awake at all?"

"The man who found him said he was conscious at first and then he couldn't wake him up. He didn't move him, thought it best to wait for the ambulance. It wasn't easy to get to him."

"I'm going over there."

Lucy nodded and her hand slipped from his arm. "Mamie is going to need some help."

"I'll make sure things get taken care of."

He headed to his truck as she got in her car and turned around. He couldn't wrap his mind around it. Ben was about the best rider around. He'd had some crashes over the years, a broken bone or two, but nothing like this.

When he pulled up to the Stillwater place it looked like the whole town was there. He hurried up the steps and didn't bother knocking. He met Tyler Grainger inside the front door.

"Tyler, how is he?"

Tyler shook his head. "Hasn't regained consciousness since the first, when they found him."

"Mamie?"

Tyler indicated with a nod that she was in the living room. "She's strong as ever. I made her let me check her vitals. She's getting ready to head to the hospital, but they have to find someone to take care of that baby."

"How is the baby?"

"I'm going to check him before I leave."

Carson and Tyler walked into the living room together. Lucy had arrived and she was sitting with Mamie.

"He must have had a momma who loves him," Mamie said, holding a blanket in her hands. She lifted the quilt. "It says Cody. That was my late husband, the twins' grandfather's, name. I'm just not sure what to do."

Lucy reached for Mamie's hand. "We'll all be here to help you. And we'll figure out who his father is."

Carson looked away from Mamie as Eva Brooks entered the room with the baby in her arms. She didn't look like the most comfortable female holding that fussing baby against her shoulder, a bottle in her hand. Carson's attention shifted to Tyler Grainger. He'd stood and was heading Eva's way. To examine the baby, of course. Maybe to rescue the poor little guy. As Eva handed over the baby in what had to be the most awkward pass ever, Tyler laughed a little and leaned close to Ben's cousin.

"I'm going to need to go to the hospital." Mamie stood. "And of course we'll need a nanny for that little mite. A baby can be a real handful, and I'm not as young as I used to be. Ben is just going to have to get himself better and get home to take care of this mess."

"He will, Mamie, he will." Lucy hugged Mamie. "Let me drive you to the hospital."

Carson helped the older woman out to Lucy's car, leaving Tyler and Eva to handle little Cody, or Ben Junior, until something else could be figured out. After Mamie was situated, Lucy shook her head.

"Identical twin brothers. A DNA test isn't going to solve this. But I don't think that matters right now. We have to pray Ben gets better soon."

And then she was gone, lights flashing as she went down the driveway.

Carson headed out to the barn to make sure the hands who were on site knew what needed to be done until Ben could get home.

Ben would get home. He said a prayer as he walked, Ben's dog chasing along behind him.

He was about ready for at least one day to go right. He thought about Ruby and how much better this day would be if he had her to sit down and talk to. If he had her to hold on to.

Chapter Seventeen

Nothing felt right that evening. Sitting at the table with Brandon and Jenna should have felt right. They were a family, having dinner the way families do. Carson pushed back his plate and rubbed a hand down his face. He was bone tired.

"Go talk to her."

He looked up at his sister's words. "What?"

"Ruby. Go talk to her. You've been pacing around here like a lion with a thorn in his paw. Go to Ruby. Get this mess straightened out. Act like adults and work—"

He raised a hand. "You do not get to give me relationship advice."

She grinned. "Well, I do know what it takes to make a marriage fall apart. Selfishness, not talking, spending too much time apart."

"Like I said, not a marriage expert."

"We've both failed, big brother. But you have a chance to make this right. It isn't your fault or Ruby's that your family did everything they could to tear the two of you apart."

He stood, still amazed at how interfering his family could be. Even today. Interfering. "I'm going."

"To Ruby's?" Brandon looked up. "Can I go?"

Jenna pointed to his plate. "You have green beans to eat. Uncle Carson has crow to eat."

"Crow?" Brandon made a disgusted face. "That's gross."

Carson mouthed "thank you" to his sister and headed for the front door. But first he made a pit stop in his office. A man had to go into battle armed and ready.

When he got to the Donovan place he saw lights on in the barn and Ruby's silhouette moving inside the old building. He pulled his truck out there and stopped. Ruby moved to see who had shown up. She waved and went back to work.

"How is Ben? Any news?" she asked when he walked into the barn.

"Nothing new. I called on my way over. He's still unconscious."

"I'm sorry. Really sorry. Gran and I prayed for him. We're praying for a miracle." She brushed long strokes across the horse's back. "What about the baby? Have they called family services? As relatives they can get a kinship placement."

"I think Lucy called it in."

"Good. If they need help, let me know."

"I will." He reached for her hand and the brush she kept sliding across the same spot on the horse's back, making the animal twitch. "Stop."

He took the brush and tossed it in the bucket. "Stop brushing the horse. Stop talking about other people. Stop running from us."

"I'm not running. I'm just..." She shook her head. "I'm tired."

"Me, too." He untied the horse and led him to a stall. "I'm tired of being alone. I'm tired of not having you next to me."

"Carson—"

He placed a finger on her lips and she quieted.

"Today a good friend of mine got hurt. He's in a hospital in critical condition. And when I found out, I wanted you. I wanted to talk to you and lean on you."

"I'm sorry I wasn't there." She came to him then, wrapping her arms around him. "I'm sorry."

Her head was against his chest and her arms

were tight around his waist. Man, she felt so good there against his heart. He held on to her. He kissed the top of her head and she looked up. He wanted to kiss her. He briefly touched his lips to hers. Just briefly.

"Why are you here?" she asked.

"To tell you I'm sorry. For what my dad did. For what Jenna did. For not coming after you years ago and asking what happened. And I'm sorry that I let you leave the other night because we should have talked then. We have a bad habit, you and I, of not talking things out."

"What is there to say?"

"There's a lot to say, Ruby. We could start with sorry. We could start by saying we won't always agree. Sometimes we'll have differences of opinion. We might even get mad at each other. But walking away? That's never going to happen again."

"We live such different lives," she started. "I'm not even sure if we can stay here. Iva needs more care and this place is costing me rather than supporting us."

"And again, we should talk about those things. Not run from them."

She kissed his shoulder and nodded. "You're right."

"Are you sniffing me?" He smiled as he asked.

"Yeah, I am. Because when I'm here close to you, and I smell your scent, I feel like I'm home."

"You are home." He held her tight and it was hard to breathe, hard to find the words. Because with Ruby in his arms, it was like coming home in the best possible way.

"Derek sold our dad's championship buckle. That's how he paid for Alyssa's necklace. That buckle. I've told him for years that he had to get rid of it, stop pretending that it meant everything. It was a possession, nothing more."

"And he finally found something that meant more." Carson whispered against her hair, her sweet scented hair. "I know how he feels."

"So what do we do now?" Ruby asked. "Carson Thorn, I'm Ruby Donovan. My brother is a suspect in the local ranch thefts. We're broke. As much as we don't seem to belong in each other's lives, you will always be the Thorn that I hope God doesn't remove from my side."

He laughed at that. "Are you proposing to me, Ruby Donovan?"

Because he was not going to let her beat him to the punch.

Ruby smiled up at the man she loved more than she'd ever dreamed possible. As a girl she'd loved him because he'd made her feel accepted and special. As a woman she loved him because he made her feel whole.

"I think I am proposing," she admitted. "You used to be the Thorn I prayed God would remove. That He'd take your memory, the place you left void in my heart, and that He would help me forget and move on. But He didn't see fit to answer that prayer."

"No, He didn't. And I'm glad. Because I couldn't live without you, Ruby. I've existed since you left, but I don't think I've been living."

He leaned. His lips—firm, warm, soft—covered hers in a kiss that told her how much he'd missed her. She returned the kiss, her mouth moving to his neck. Even after all these years his scent was familiar. She wanted to stay in that place, in his arms. Forever.

Unfortunately he moved. His arms dropped from her waist and he stepped back to reach into his pocket. "I think you were fed misinformation by my sister. You overheard something about a ring and another woman."

She nodded, trying not to cry at the pain the memory evoked. Jenna's carefully placed words had devastated her.

"Yes, that's what I heard her say."

"Promise me that from now on we will talk

when you hear something or even if you doubt or have questions."

"I promise we will talk," she whispered, finding it hard to speak. Her throat felt tight with emotion.

"I did buy a ring that year." He held it out for her to see. "This ring. And I bought it intending to ask you to be my wife. I wanted to marry you, Ruby. There wasn't anyone else. There's never been anyone else. Just you."

"Carson." What else could she say? "I did this. I kept us apart."

He reached for her hand and slid the diamond solitaire on the right finger. "We did this. We're both to blame. And now we're both going to repair what was broken and reclaim what was lost. We have a lot of years to make up for, Ruby Jo Donovan."

He cupped her cheeks in strong, steady hands and leaned to kiss her again. Afterward, with his forehead resting against hers, he let his fingers trace a path down her cheeks and then his hands slid behind her neck.

"Marry me, Ruby. Be my wife. Please have my babies, because I really want a few kids."

She laughed at that. "I want little boys who look like Brandon. When I see you with him, I think about that. That we could have had a little boy like him."

"We will have a little boy like Brandon. Maybe two or three. And a girl." He kissed her again. "Is this a yes?"

She wrapped her arms around his neck. "Most definitely a yes, Carson Thorn."

"We should go tell Iva," he said.

"I wouldn't doubt that she doesn't already know. She told me this morning she's praying we come to our senses before it's too late for her to hold great grandbabies."

He led her out of the barn, turned off the lights and closed the door behind them. The surveillance cameras were on. The place was as secure as they could get it.

Thieves and town politics weren't on Ruby's mind as Carson led her down the driveway to the house she'd grown up in. That little house—not big, not fancy, but filled with love and faith.

She thought of the home they would have, the children they would fill it with. They would have love and laughter and faith. They would have hard times, too. She knew that. But they would have each other.

Forever.

* * * * *

Dear Reader,

I'm so glad you've joined us for the Lone Star Cowboy League series where you'll get to know the people of Little Horn, Texas. You'll join them as they discover love, faith and maybe a little about their own lives. You won't want to miss a book because you'll definitely want to know how it all ends for our characters! I'm thrilled that I got to write book one, introducing you all to the town and its inhabitants. I got to kick off the romance with a couple just destined to be together—even though family tried to throw a wrench in their plans. Sit back with a cup of coffee or tea, and get to know Carson Thorn and Ruby Donovan, the first couple in this exciting series.

Brenda Minton

LARGER-PRINT BOOKS!

GET 2 FREE
LARGER-PRINT NOVELS
PLUS 2 FREE
MYSTERY GIFTS

Love Inspired
SUSPENSE
RIVETING INSPIRATIONAL ROMANCE

Larger-print novels are now available...

LISLP15